LUNAR FOLLIES

by Gilbert Sorrentino

Coffee House Press

2005

COPYRIGHT © 2005 by Gilbert Sorrentino
COVER + BOOK DESIGN Linda Koutsky
COVER PHOTO © Rana K. Williamson

Coffee House Press books are available to the trade through our primary distributor, Consortium Book Sales & Distribution, 1045 Westgate Drive, Saint Paul, MN 55114. For personal orders, catalogs, or other information, write to: Coffee House Press, 27 North Fourth Street, Suite 400, Minneapolis, MN 55401.

Coffee House Press is a nonprofit literary publishing house. Support from private foundations, corporate giving programs, government programs, and generous individuals help make the publication of our books possible. We gratefully acknowledge their support in detail in the back of this book. To you and our many readers across the country, we send our thanks for your continuing support.

LIBRARY OF CONGRESS CIP DATA
Sorrentino, Gilbert.
Lunar follies / by Gilbert Sorrentino.
p. cm.
ISBN-13: 978-1-56689-169-1 (alk. paper)
ISBN-10: 1-56689-169-8 (alk. paper)
1. Art—Exhibitions—Fiction. 2. Arts—Fiction. I. Title.
PS3569.O7L86 2005
813'.54—DC22
2004028140

FIRST EDITION | FIRST PRINTING
1 3 5 7 9 8 6 4 2
Printed in Canada

Portions of this work first appeared in *McSweeney's*.

LUNAR FOLLIES

CONTENTS

" . . . while the ears, be we mikealls or nicholists, may sometimes be inclined to believe others the eyes, whether browned or nolensed, find it devilish hard now and again even to believe itself."

FINNEGANS WAKE

"You're painting a shoe; you start painting the sole, and it turns into a moon; you start painting the moon, and it turns into a piece of bread."

PHILIP GUSTON

ALPHONSUS

George Alphonsus, famed as the Supreme Master of Magic, is said to have had a hand in creating the illusion that has, quite successfully and convincingly, asserted itself as "art for our time." The question asked most frequently has been, "what of the millennium?" Or, on occasion, "what of the exciting millennium?" George *creates* the convincing illusion, which, most agree, silences the seasoned and cynical journalists, who are, of course, the framers of such questions as have to do with "art for our time." For instance: "Is baseball too slow for our ultra-busy, speeded-up, on-the-go age?" "Will the loathsome cockroach lead the way to a cure for breast cancer?" "Was John Kennedy Junior a closet queen?" "Do we have to die?" "How can we be happy in a bad job?" And "Is birth-control science the way to the Rapture?" But to the Supreme Master of Magic, anent his astonishing and artistic illusions (which, he insists, and strongly, on calling "The art of astonishing and artistic illusions"), they ask, e.g., "How does it feel, George?" Silence usually ensues, and so it's on to the snow-chains story; the heat-wave story; the

story of the tough coach and his swell young protégé; the
killer-hurricane (with puppy) story; the mudslide story
and the people who will rebuild; the forest-fire story and
the people who will rebuild; the flash-flood story and the
people who will rebuild; the depraved priest story and the
youths he abused every night for nine years; and, of
course, the magnificent new stadium that will seat
150,000, cost nothing, make an entire city rich, and stamp
out the cocaine trade as well, so that the little guy, if white,
will win at least maybe story. And all the while, through
rain and fog and the golden California sun that bakes the
brain right through the jaunty baseball caps that are always
the rage, George, the Supreme Master of Magic's, newest
illusion is, yes, right this way, over here, yes, here you go,
right by the spilled latte, yes: illusion dot com dot magic-
george dot com you chumps.

ALPINE VALLEY

The place or space or venue is rife or blossoming with pictures or photographs or collages or photocollages of the famous avant-garde publisher's wife, the famous underground diva or fringe dancer or performance artist, whose most renowned and transgressive "happening"—as such events were termed in the sixties in all their rude and feverish innocence and glamour—"Cunnus Delicti," concluded with the artist slowly pulling a long, thin scroll of paper from her vagina. In between periods of "whirlwind creativity," as her husband smilingly notes, she likes to read the submissions that come in over the transom, as they occasionally say in publishing. This spousal remark is recorded, in its totality, amid the images that virtually surround one in the studio, amid a clash of vital forms. One novel was thought to be too long for its fragile premise, yet the choreographic instincts that inform the artist's "mind" are too present ever to permit her to define the word "premise." This has always been her way, so says her adoring husband, from behind his aromatically billowing briar. "She has an eye for the authentic,"

he is quoted as saying in a yellowing, brittle newspaper clip-
ping, the words glowing with orange highlighter ink or solution or is it, perhaps, a kind of water color? Above this focal
point, or "coign," as a dear old friend from "boardwalk days"
has called it, this endearing remark, virtually palpable in its
compassion for the real, the authentic, the unashamedly
human, is a photograph of the artist, in her *defining moment,*
pulling the paper scroll from her proud, naked vagina; and, just
above the photograph, sharing the wall space that overlooks
the massive worktable crammed, as always, with ideas for new
dances, new performance ideas, new and startling contor-
tions, just above it, stained, creased, covered with admirers'
notes of congratulation and admiration, and, forebodingly,
warning, like a stern aegis, or a harbinger of just what art can
be, is the discolored scroll itself, assertive, defiant!

ALPS

Terrifying photographs, drawings, and poor collages of "Old Geordy Sime," one of his era's most famous pipers, alternate with miniature reproductions of the Alard Stradivarius, the installation, a word nicely borrowed from the Persian (like "peach"), creating a kind of frieze that dominates the small and warmly claustrophobic room. The title of this particular installation is "Welsh Harps," an oblique *hommage* to Sime. The artist's irrepressible sense of humor is everywhere apparent here. The portrayed women defend their actualities in no uncertain terms, here on the cutting edge. "They'll no longer take 'no' for an answer," would seem to be the essential rubric under which deft revolutions occur; and then there is "neon is their middle name," another call to arms. The word "cunt" may not, of course, be used, save in the correct, life-affirming way. Indian drums are scattered about, if drums can ever be "scattered." Yet scattered they joyously are, in the ineluctable ways of craft, and craft is all, when you get right down to it. It's time that artists who aren't pulling their own weight were given the bum's rush.

"The Bum's Rush" is, fortuitously, the overall title of the whole exhibit. Over on the other wall is the interior profile of an English church organ, which completes the diorama— calling capitalism, once more, to account. Dioramas, as presented by certain fabled buildings at the 1939 World's Fair in Flushing Meadows, Queens, New York, were sublimely vulgar and made kitsch into the "art of our time." "Atwill's Musical Establishment" was first seen in the Yerba Buena Gardens in San Francisco, but was withheld from this particular show by those few who *know*. A wild twangling daily issues forth from all corners of the "space": at one, three, and five P.M. "Ring dem bells!" is the wonted cry from the poets who get five free tickets each day, starting at noon. (This is not the Director's doing!) Poets are likely to do just about anything for a buck, as they say, or for publication in *Zing, Edelweiss Review, Insomnia News, Hurdygurdy, Blotto,* and *The Tribes*. "Their hurts healed for a few dollars" or two contributor's copies. On Tuesdays, senior citizens are admitted at half-price, God love them.

ALTAI SCARP

Here are the stars of eternity, some dressed as imitation ladies. In attendance, two-inch engineers, cut out of cardboard, and curious in transparent socks. The sun, which shines on the tableau, is red, and, as usual, round, something like the dial of a watch. The stars, it should be noted, cluster about a red table upon which are displayed a wooden spool that apparently once held thread, a scatter of paper clips, a tin airplane, and a few old elastics, or, as they are usually called, "rubber bands." These items may, possibly, be glued to the table's surface. There is, too, an unappetizing dinner rather carelessly crowded onto a small area of the table, where it has grown stone cold. In a corner of the room, a trunk, leather and lined with leather, ready for the stars' vacation, is "gummed" all over with red stars and small photographs of tables and trunks; and next to it are its trays, removed so as to display their contents, nothing more than a number of hinged boxes, filled, almost overflowing, with small discs of white cardboard edged with nickeled metal of some sort. Each disc has the same words carefully inscribed, in red ink, on one side: DARN, CONVEY, DISCOVER, SUCK; and on the other side: FASTER, TISSUE. It appears that the stars, or in any event those stars dressed as imitation ladies, refuse to examine or, for that matter, even glance at these "messages," and that they will continue to refuse to do so.

APPENNINES

A group, a line, actually, of determinedly, even aggressively unlifelike mannequins are arrayed, or lined up, against a ghastly backdrop of what is meant to be a Hawaiian sunset. The mannequins, male and female alike, have "breasts," and a disturbing, large sign, ANOTHER NAIL IN THE COFFIN OF BOURGEOIS GENDER ROLES, in magenta neon or something glowing, shines upon them. The mannequins appear to be dressed, or partially dressed—depending on how each mannequin is situated as a "radical construct"—as investment bankers, venture capitalists, bond traders, arbitragers, and cocksuckers, each "construct" attended by a "wife," "husband," "lover," or "partner," appropriately dressed for daily tasks and plain fun. Music plays continually on a loop (?), to the annoyance of the gallery visitors; and although this music is extremely bad, it must be noted that it is not precisely music, but *world music,* and its infirm quality a mocking comment on inverse canon formation. One mannequin, whose "breasts" are quite enormous, seems to have an equally enormous "erection" in its tight Tonetti briefs, although the flashing strobe lights that accompany the passionate if off-key strains of a "white-bread" version of a classic Venezuelan *fanfanzanga,* may well be responsible for a "bulge" that is really not there, but is an optical illusion. The noise in the gallery space is so loud as to be painful and disorienting, and this may account for the lewd, even depraved acts visited upon the mannequins by ironic and rebellious iconoclasts at virtually all hours. Such acts have come to be called, by their perpetrators and would-be perpetrators, "rudiments of gesture."

ARCHIMEDES

Piles of wet clothing, puddles of dirty, soapy water, and a tarnished crown of false, or fool's gold, set the tone for this installation, one which slowly and almost imperceptibly turns from the innocuous to the eerily disturbing, as the vast floor of the converted gymnasium, which serves as the gallery's exhibition space, accommodates, insistently and obsessively, more piles of clothing, more puddles of water, more cheap-jack crowns. It is only when the eye refuses to be mesmerized by neurotic uniformity and repetition that the floor space between these strangely iconic and wholly sterile elements of a useless formalism is seen to contain cluttered configurations of miniature, varicolored, metallic spheres, cylinders, fulcrums, circles, conoids, spheroids, ovoids, and ingeniously designed sand-reckoners. These familiar geometrical shapes function as footnotes or margin-alia, of course. The floor is bathed in a cold, aqueous, silvery light, which has the uncanny effect of making these simple conjugations of *things* (and what is more "thinglike" than laundry, wet floors, "Coney Island" headgear?) into noble, if threatening, constructions. The entire installation suggests to the viewer willing to connect with its sublunary symbolism a world—our own world, perhaps—and the number of grains of sand in their trillions upon trillions that it would take to completely fill it. An extraordinarily compelling architecture of delights, this, by the Grupo Archimedes, rich with the unspoken and unrevealed.

Eureka Downtown, through June 15th

ARISTOTELES

Two copulative verbs, large, and by nature rough, converge upon a blushing noun, which tries, gamely, to hold its skirts down in the blustery wind blowing hard toward the famed copse of eucalyptus trees imported from the Pulitzer Bank, sadly fished out long, long ago, by fascists of foreign persuasions, mostly Norwegians, drunk, and foul with innocent-whale blubber. A dreadnought hovers nearby, fly agape, yet he *seems,* at first glance, to be slipping edgewise toward the empty booth in the diner. The diner is a perfect replica of an authentic copy reconstructed from the edges of the dreams of those who know what real rock-and-roll is, and, more importantly, what it *used to be.* The entire tableau, if one may be forgiven such an evangelistic word, seems to present a kind of "truth"—and, surely, the place cards have no reason to lie, to paraphrase the professor. In his latest book on seemingly inconsequential ("yet alarmingly labile," as he notes on more than one occasion) and neglected things, he plumbs the depths of the notably banal, as this word was understood in Victorian London, and comes to many conclusions about

British comestibles. Be that as it may, the tableau keeps turning, twisting, changing, metamorphosing, and so on and so forth, over and over, in subtle homage to various geniuses of dramaturgy, post-Aristoteles, e.g.: Inigo Jones, Bob Jones, Bill Jones, Henry Jones, "Dem" Bones, August Strindberg, Irving Thalberg, Hank Greenberg, Mrs. Goldberg, "Bob" Altman, B. Altman, Bergdorf Goodman, "Noodles" Goodman, Aristotle, Richard Tottel, Dr. Fell, and others too numerous to name. But now the noun succumbs to the crass importunings of the verbs and their lusty rods* hold sway! A card appears from out of a haze of bluish smoke and on the card is lettered, "Handlome il al handlome doel," yet another trope of the colonized mind. In the careless iconography of the streets, this phrase may mean that [she] is in the process "of getting [her] ashes hauled." There is, finally, a somewhat banjaxed and vafunculed series of half-hearted alarums before Bottom enters and puts out the lights, much to the annoyance of the person hired to perform this act. This, too, is to be considered part of the shifting, flexible, ceaselessly variegated piece. "So we beat off," a volunteer demigod chuckles softly, as he leans on the windowsill to gaze at the traffic far below in the gathering summer dusk, headlights gleaming off the wet, shining streets, reading his index card with admirable precision and a degree of panache, even.

---

*The phrase, "lusty rods," may be added to the performance piece at the discretion of those who have the money, as always; but it should be made clear that the phrase is being employed with the understanding that it is ideally understood as an unconscious sexual reference, like "candy," "jelly jelly," "pussyfoot," or "bingo."

CARPATHIANS

Most serious gallery-goers of the seventies pretend to remember Moss Kuth, one of the earliest practitioners—some would say the avatar—of Exoconceptualism. This, his first exhibition in almost fifteen years, gathers well-known, to some revered, devices, and what the artist calls "plannings," those strangely occulted, iconoclastic conglomerates that heralded the end of the stasis imposed upon the art of the fifties and sixties by market-corrupted confections of pop art, op art, numero art, subway art, and the moribund rigidities of a humorless politico-expressionism. There are included, too, some recent, surprisingly sunny (though no less pointed) constructions. Moss and his wife, Magda, have been living quietly in their small farmhouse in Provence, venturing only as far as Paris once or twice a year to stock up on books, visit the galleries, and spend a convivial evening or two with such old ghosts as Matisse, Picasso, and Gris, "quarreling," as Magda smilingly puts it, "the night away." In the large and breathtaking photo by Dan Ray that dominates the gallery's south wall, Moss, Magda, and their

Irish wolfhound, Lummox, are revealed, all three dressed in hip, severe black, amid the prize-winning roses that have endeared Magda to the world of horticulture, as that word is grotesquely understood in the very seat of Gallic culture. The show itself is simple, austere, elegant: a collection of letters from friends and enemies; wide-ranging commentary—favorable, vicious, perceptive, stupid, toadying—on certain passages in the letters, from over twenty years' worth of Kuthian studies and criticism; the criticism, in full, itself; Kuth's remarks on the studies, the criticism, and the commentary on the commentary on the letters; a jumbled display of Kuth's tattered notebooks, containing alternative commentary on the commentary on the letters; a blank notebook, its pages fanned out, provocatively perched upon a ream of cheap white paper; and a small black-and-white snapshot of Magda, playfully sucking Moss off under the pines at Yaddo, often called "the Yaddo pines." Located at the extreme edges of the display are letters from both Kuth and Magda to each other, stained with what appears to be dog shit, agreeing with all the negative commentary on Kuth's work, and wholly composed in crude, ungrammatical, trite, and shrewdly misspelled English, an English, as Magda has impishly noted, "that is hours all own."

CATHARINA

High upon a wall, quite near the ceiling, a large thing, colored a strangely glowing puce, abuts a frosty moon.
Splinters descend, *splinters of ice,* falling on other things
below; below, that is to say, the frosty moon's "mirror
image" (although this notion has long been subject to critical attack, mostly labile in nature), the thunder moon. The
latter moon leans against a lavender thing. Other vaguely
organic elements crowd about, in the best possible way.
Piled in an attractive heap down by the entrance to the
pongee grouping, flanked, as tradition demands, by metallic
pillars crafted in homage to Catharina Duchesse, the old
Caliph's favorite filly, are variously sized, smoldering exam-
ples of perfectly designed representations of a grass moon,
egg moon, planting moon, milk moon, rose moon, flower
moon, strawberry moon, hay moon, green corn moon,
grain moon, fruit moon, hunger's moon, and a beaver
moon, disguised as a spruce moon, in honor of the Yuletide
season. Above this gleaming jumble of dazzling color and
sparkling surface hangs the always reliable harvest moon,

which shines on, shines on. In a revealing photograph of the old Hotel Astor, things appear to have got somewhat out of hand. The hotel band, Tab Jazzetti and His Melodists, seems to be trying to "swing," or so it would seem from close observation of the musicians' divers postures. Their music stands mysteriously bear the initials OO, said initials being intertwined and dusted with mica so as to glitter like the *frosty moon*. It's best when the sun strikes the whole dance floor, so they say, with a kind of rousing BANG, although incandescent lighting will do in a pinch, that is, on a dark day. Fluorescent lights, however, really mess things up rather badly. "Might as well not be here at all with the moons looking like that," some have been overheard to say from the polished floor. And many of them were quite respectably dressed, and, it is rumored, know all the best restaurants. Wherein, sad to say, the fucking morons always order the *wrong things*.

CΛUCΛSUS MOUΠTΛIΠS

The Odradek, the first one to be placed on public view in the United States in more than a century, has been, we are told in the helpful catalogue, prepared by Tobias Blumfeld for the Prague Zoological Society and Marching Band, "preserved . . . in what analysis shows to be a solution of equal parts hydrogen peroxide, lemon juice, and triple-distilled 160 proof Ukrainian vodka." Discovered three years ago in a grotto in the Caucasus, the small creature has been seen, and marveled at, in museums the world over, before his arrival in this country earlier in the year. From here, the Odradek will travel back to what will be his permanent home in Azerbaijan's National Wool Museum. Although the bits and pieces of thread, tangled together, as always, that are wound about the little creature are varied in color, as we have come to expect, these threads seem remarkably *new;* that is to say, one expects, somehow, the Odradek to display "raiment" that is as old as himself—and star-scholars agree that this particular specimen is between 800 and 1,100 years old. For the Odradek to flaunt threads newly manufactured when *he* was already centuries old diminishes the little being's "presence," of course. One hastens to add, however, that this diminishment is neither profound nor, finally, important. As a matter of fact, the colors of the threads (azure, rose, chartreuse, burnt orange, alabaster, pearl grey, butter, and lavender) are so striking as to constitute an authentic, enduring beauty as they flutter against the matte, off-black contours of the Odradek's five-pointed body, and the dull mahogany of his crossbar with its cunningly attached rod. The little creature stands upright and utterly still on his wooden rod and one of his star points or "legs," although it is apparently possible for him to heave himself onto his dorsal surface, despite the fact that no one has ever seen him do so; nor has anyone ever seen the little fellow resting in what may be thought of as a supine position. Viewers gaze long upon the Odradek, fascinated by his curious, modest charm. Most, when queried, admit that they are beginning to hear him speak; according to mountain legend, the Odradek's lightest word is able to change his hearers' lives forever.

CLAVIUS

Rejected Works: Otto Clavius Contemporaries

"Slightly Menacing Shadows," Jeanne Souze; "Luminous White Dresses," Emiliano Soreau; "The Snowman, His Tiny Eyes Glittering," Isidor Martin; "A Wife, or Was She a Whore?," Donald Chainville; "Blue Enamel Bulb," Ann Jenn; "Barely Moving On," Russell Cuiper; "Cigarette Hysteria," Emilia Sladky; "Lost Items of Clothing," Bill Juillard; "Depraved Scenes of Village Life," Leonard Bacon; "Amid a Cloud of White," Ronald LeFlave; "The Holocaust of Books," Edward Carmichael; "Refinements of the Baroque," Stephen Alcott; "The Far Side of the Lake," Isabella Stella; "Freak Cartoons," Ivan Hounsfield; "The Blue Hamper," Jonathan Tancred; "The Distinguished Publisher," Ström Owns; "Fragments of Malarkey," J. Branch Bex; "Evidence of Pain and Anger," Ramp St. James; "Life-Sized Doll," Harlow Warbucks; "Molten Blue Metal," Jed Whag; "Tin Pig Behind the Door," Frank Hector; "Cuisine Noire," Cassandra Ballesteros; "Wading in the Shallows," Sandor Skariofszky; "The Carnal Jitters," Bridget Agostin; "Her Fiancé's Mother and Two Older Sisters," Sydelle Lelgach; "Translucent

Spheroids," Marcus Tommie; "Distant Female Figures in White," Gregory Balbet; "The Maddening Cassandra," Bart Ballesteros; "The Long Bitter Night Was a Snowy One," Olga Chervonen; "The Delights of Housework," Claudia Bedu; "Myrna Felt Like Undressing for the Conductor," Yolanda Philippo; "The Meaning of the Past," Claude Urbane; "Wife of an Adulterous Banker," Claire Hounsfield; "The Storage of Gardening Equipment," Moko; "The Great Sculptor," Archibald Fuxer; "Closed Door of Thick Blue Steel," Joshua Bex; "A Pathetic Attempt at Comedy," Barbara Frietchie; "Two Spectral White Trees," Robert Bedu; "Maddened, Quarreling, Screaming Crowd," Claude Luxo; "Sweet Guilt," Norman Bob; "Three Determined Strokes of Cadmium White," John Cerjet; "World of Chips," Sheldon Marius; "Glossy Black Chinese Teapot," Caleb Bex; "Onrush of Twilight," Solange McCarty; "Unwanted Reflections," Hubert-Allen Zipp; "Jaded Desk Clerk," Lafcadio Bob; "Bottle of Worcestershire Sauce," Raoul; "The Brilliance of the Moon," Luigi Borsalino; "The Murky Stage of His Recollections," Corporal Hitler; "Clothed in Gleaming White," Theodore Rosa-Rose; "Three Young Women of About Seventeen," Alex Found; "A Flash of White," Ursula Grüntéd; "A Panel of Christian Experts," Senator Weep; "Navy Blue Melton Overcoat," Emilie Bex; "Girl in the Cellar," Rondee; "Helga, the Hermit Ghost," Benno DeLux; "Too Good to Be True," Gain Doyle; "Three Women in Newspaper Hats," Ford Hills; "This Vast Desire," Willis Took.

Open 24 Hours, Through December 18th, No Photos!

CLEOMEDES

These are portraits and busts of Cleomedes, "Eddie C," created from imagination, fantasy, sketchy and unsatisfactory biographies, and forged records, not to mention suspect memories and poorly written yet loathsomely reverent memoirs (which recall Céline's dry remark, "every virtue has its contemptible literature"), and the anecdotes of friends and enemies, all of whom are rather sweatily trying, as they say, to look their best. So then, whatever his true visage, it will not be found here, that seems certain. More interesting, at least to some, is that in about the year 125, we are told, Cleomedes had the radical idea that the earth is round and that the moon, when full, is actually the face of a bloated, imbecilic, and acne-scarred God. His inability to explain the moon's weird shapes in its other "phases" made him, or so a contemporary memoir suggests, a "figure of fun." Cleomedes also worked as a creative consultant on such songs as "Carolina Moon," "The Moon Is Blue," "Moonlight Serenade," "Moon River," "On Moonlight Bay," "Moon Love," "Moonglow," "Moon Over Miami," "Moonlight Becomes

You," "The Moon of Manakoora," "Alabama Song," "Moonlight on the Ganges," "Moonlight and Roses," "The Moon Was Yellow," "Moonlight in Vermont," "Moonlight Cocktail," "Blues My Naughty Sweetie Gives to Me," "The Daughter of Rosie O'Grady," and "Why Do They All Take the Night Boat to Albany?". The smallest of eleven busts, hammered out of a matte-nickel alloy, shows him smiling somewhat sardonically, if not cruelly. Most neo-historicist theorists as well as critics of trenchant opinions agree that this unassuming piece is as close as we are likely to come to an accurate depiction of "Eddie C," for it has been generally accepted that the figure shown is caught in the moment before singing, or, perhaps, chanting, "O moon of Alabama, we now must say goodbye." At the very least, this essentially pedestrian exhibition allows the patient visitor a chance to appreciate the "home truths" and mending walls, so to speak, behind the bias of the structuralist radicalization of representational male iconography, no small feat, especially when it is realized that there is but one bathroom on the floor and that one "Out Of Order."

COPERNICUS

A Collage

On a kind of moor, as it is called in England, there sits a castle, much the worse for the neglect of centuries, within which a small band of elderly men regularly discuss the elements of natural philosophy, while toying each with his soap-bubble set. These sets are unusual, to say the least, configured, as each is, of a glass ball and a star game, the latter secretly manufactured, or so it is rumored, in either the Palace Hotel or the Golden Key Hotel, both located in Jersey City, New Jersey, a city which Max Ernst (or perhaps Tristan Tzara) called a "surrealist box," an odd cognomen for a city best known for its extraordinarily lascivious, not to say obscene portraits of the lewd twins, Ondine and Rose Hobart. Some of the elderly men occasionally mutter of the lost bookstalls of Fourth Avenue in Old Manahatta, which, some aver, they frequented every night with, as one likes to shout in a cracked, phlegmy voice, "torch and spear!" Another, almost invariably, begins, at this precise moment, to read, for the first of three or four times, *The Children's Party,* a "compelling, compulsively readable" memoir of a man who humped not only his sister and his mother, but did so as a practicing, militant homosexual, a member of the Republican Party of Alabama, and a storied bore.

"A Legend for Fountains," a portrait of the castle's original tenant, Sir Joshua Nymphlight, has been well-nigh obliterated by the dirt, soot, and smoke of centuries, which may be, or so the jape goes, all to the good, seeing that Sir Joshua dreamed the forbidden aviary dream, that fearsome dream sometimes known as "the green dream," "the fairy dream," or, most often, here on the windswept moor, "Jack's dream." There are stories still told by rosy, and, of needs, dancing fireplace light, of the riotous midnights, the hearts on velvet sleeves, and the unspeakable services rendered Sir Joshua and his rakehell friends by Tilly Losch, one of the famous whores of indeterminate sex of that corrupt era we now call by the simple yet ominous term, the "Object Era." Pharmacies, or what we now know as pharmacies, but which were then simple "egypts," did a stupendously lucrative business when the crazed whoremongers and their bawds and morphodites—under contract to Mrs. Losch—spilled forth from Sir Joshua's chambers of sin and perversion to avail themselves of salves and poultices to still the burning of the "codpiece fever," as Ben Jonson termed it, that consumed them. These revelers christened the castle the Pink Palace, and in later years, the sounds of timbrel and calliope, of lute and viola da scuccia and bonzophone emanating from the fabled pile in the rendition of such airs as "Follow Thy Faire Sunne," "Baby Marie," and "Oh You Beautiful Doll" drove the livestock, for miles around, into that special frenzy peculiar to England and all things English, from their crown jewels and greasy bangers to their derby days and dumb Irish jokes.

During the long evenings and longer nights of droning argument and wayward discussion among the elderly sages, bumpkins, reprobates, drunks, and others who comprised "the Group," as the castle's devotees of unabashed sloth were thought of by the bemused if essentially moronic townspeople, Paul and Virginia often frequented one of the small shire's penny arcades, the one, incidentally, that featured—proudly—three vaguely perverse portraits of Lauren Bacall in her salad days: one as a Medici princess, one as a Medici prince, and one as a Medici commoner. The background, in each of these depictions of the famed star, was, so the portraitist was supposedly heard to say, the Hôtel du Cygne in Paris, the deluxe establishment that had been the dream and triumph of Mrs. Spyros Apollinaris, and that patterned the configurations of its rooms and suites on that lady's manipulations of her specially designed "solar set," a kind of ultrasophisticated ouija board that was the final creation of Rose des Vents, the celebrated fundraiser, artisan, marathon runner, and secret cocksucker to the stars, who was, to one and all in the demimonde, Mademoiselle Cassiopeia.

Paul and Virginia almost always found themselves, toward dawn, in the corner of the penny arcade known as the Grand Owl Habitat, a curious name for what was, in essence, a shooting gallery that had been rescued from the ruins of the Hotel Eden, a rambling apartment hotel designed, for some reason, now lost to students of the faux baroque, to look like the Pink Palace. The curious targets in the gallery were somewhat crude depictions, almost caricatures, of Juan Gris and his parrot, Griselda; the Grand Hotel Semiramis (where Jean Cocteau is said to have been surreptitiously "born again" into heterosexuality); and a miniature model of the Blue Peninsula, complete with its legendary corks and narcotic newspaper prose. Virginia almost always tried to hit each kind of target, the prize for success in this endeavor a cheap rhinestone tiara that had once belonged to Missy Vanessa, the "whore princess" of Omaha, or a hand-colored plate, imaging, in amateurish bas-relief, some sort of unrecognizable animal surrounded by infirm representations of a spavined horse, a sinking schooner, and a Chinese bottle with a dancing grasshopper inside its narrow fastness. "The Mooch," who managed the arcade, a man known to many as the Ice Traveler, would show Virginia, and Paul as well, after Virginia's inevitable, one might say predictable failure of marksmanship, a thimble forest with beehive, as perhaps, a consolation prize, and smilingly, or, as Paul thought, leeringly, call her the "Snow Maiden." "Where's the book with the marble," Paul would ask, almost as if instructed to do so, "John Donne's keepsake?" But there was, of course, no "book with the marble," as Paul well knew. The Mooch, who greatly disliked Paul because of the young man's obvious intimacy with Virginia, would offer him, in lieu of this imaginary "book," a book with a *window,* a dressing-room for exhibitionists, a pantry ballet, and Jacques Offenbach's last cheese carton, one made of wood and perfect for holding scores of baseball cards. Strained laughter ensued.

As this nocturnal adventure ran its course, as it did on many evenings, within the confines of the penny arcade, the elders in the castle set their gaming tables in preparation for an evening of Black Hunter, a version of the Korean board game of great antiquity, Box with Corks and Other Corks. The winner of the previous month's marathon match would dress himself in the clothing which closely imitated that worn by Rose Castle, the semi-mythical madam of the brothel known, as far back as the Crusades, as Taglioni's Jewel Casket; and a romantic ballet, homophobically yet courageously perverse in its brutal choreography, would be performed by "Rose Castle" atop a souvenir case wheeled in by the masked men affectionately called "The Little Mysteries." This band of assistants had been in charge of wheeling the souvenir case here and there, whenever and wherever required, for as long as anyone could remember, as far back, as a matter of fact, as the castle's moldering records went. Then the game began, its opening always the same, the traditional, staid, yet excruciatingly impenetrable and inexplicable move that had been christened, by Mad King Ludwig and The Three Musketeers, "Glass in Naples." As the game progressed, a parlor constellation, with both rattle and music box, was softly illuminated by two beautiful maids who were always known as Emily One and Emily Two. The Emilys would, at times, at the direction of a particularly playful elder, add a sand fountain that had graced Apollinaire's Cuban mansion to the display, and sometimes, too, a slot machine that was believed by some to be the handiwork of the beautiful Caravaggio.

While the game moved forward and backward in its ineluctable and darkly mysterious way, Paul and Virginia, wandering through the area abutting the by-now deserted penny arcade, gawked at strangers shoot the chutes, their screams of delighted fear as cheering to the young couple as sweet childhood's sunbox of Golden Delicious apples and the *bel canto* of the youthful tenor whose stage name was "the Caliph of Baghdad." Then they were off to the Midway and the pleasures of sideshow attractions like the parrot with a beak of chocolate, the robotic weather prophet and his talking yellow durgh, the eerie habitats of extinct and loathsome marine life, and a cage crammed with representative poems on the sheer greatness of American Gothic thought and prayer. Descartes' dovecote, a new attraction obscurely named "Starbox with Starfish," was not quite what the couple expected, and after a time, they stopped in to the Trade Winds, a café and inn whose Longitude Suite was "just what the doctor ordered," as Donald E. Mobile, the cutting-edge *scripteur,* once remarked in his astonishing critical prose. Virginia particularly liked the three-dimensional panorama of the sun rising, the sun setting, and days and nights of temperate beauty; while Paul was attracted to the video representations of the phases of the moon and selected cosmography elements, all of which quite mysteriously became one with the nuclear atom and its space object, which, quite unnervingly, seemed to be the night skies above the Grand Universal Hotel. The latter edifice—although this was not known to Paul and Virginia—was, or perhaps one should say, *is,* absolutely identical to the castle on the moor, within which the game of Black Hunter was now in its fifth hour. It had reached that moment of transformation called *Central Park carousel pavilion,* a critical juncture that always nullified the effects of the aggressive gambit, *American Gothic casement,* even when that move was followed by the spectacular *night sky and window façade.*

"A Broken Window," a string quartet by Dirk Giotto, woke Paul and Virginia from their lovers' sleep, a sleep that had served as the coda to their tender but filthy amours, which, at this time, in any event, had been based on "Circe and Her Lovers in 'Mathematics in Nature,'" a famous short story especially composed for the people of the castle, the café, the palace, and the Isle of Children. "The puzzle of the reward," Paul said, as he and Virginia dressed, "is the sister shade." Virginia smiled. "Home, poor heart, home," she said, softly, and their slightly loony remarks constituted, at least for them, an allegory of innocence. At this precise moment, one of the Black Hunter players realized that *ship with nude,* a devastating, crushing move, was possible for him to make, perhaps even possible doubled, as *Robinson Crusoe and his blue nude dream.* He lifted his hand, moved his platinum counters and his vegetable tiles, and time, transfixed as if to make a rainbow, ceased for a split second, and created, as someone obscurely remarked, years later, a virtual aerodynamics for *Allegra's valentine.* "That's the only way I can put it," this someone added. For that split second, *Pascal's triangle* and *constellations of autumn* were "trumped," so to speak, by the possessed player's deployment of the uncertainty principle. Watching the game, a smoker of chocolate, wearing a derby hat, was the first to realize that Paul and Virginia, two shadowy icons forever hidden within the very "machinery" of the game, had suddenly made their board appearance, if such a term may be used for such an uncanny occurrence. It was a sign to all that the game was about to take a turn toward the arrest of entropic forces. A small cheer went up as Paul and Virginia assumed control, tentatively, from the hands of the last Prince of Urbino, long exiled in Babylon.

CORDILLERA MOUNTAINS

High Concept Men, High Country Fashion

DAVID APOLLO: *Celebrity and kitchenware photographer;* Three-button wool, abraded burlap and faux-orlon suit, $15,450 and "dirty" ramie and oilcloth shirt, $450. At Barron's Ice Company. GORDY JERICHO: *Fine-art and broken-furniture embosser;* Eight-button disappearing pinstripe crushed-wool suit, $9,050. At Barchas-Willin. ELPASO JOHNSON: *Backyard and high-school-athlete sketch artist;* Four-button leather and corrugated paper jacket, $6,000 and nylon "Good Humor" pants, $1,250. At Sapp and Patsy. MANNY TOUCHANT: *Vintage guitar and ketchup-bottle repair technician;* Aged cashmere and celluloid pullover, $1,200, from Tommy Cafone. At Tommy Cafone. JUBAL OCTUBRE: *Retail-outlet and velvet-animal planning analyst;* Ink-stained cotton T-shirt, $450 and recycled-glass "midnight" jeans, $385. At Stroonz. BYRON VAN HAKKA: *Vegetable and celebrity garbage-and-excrement photographer;* Smashed cotton quarter-shirt, $605 and wool and rhinoceros-hide pants, $11,250. At Paco Coño. COLTRANE MARTINES: *Horse-lover and movie-goer;* Food-encrusted and fake rayon-blend sweater, $900. At Caponato USA. FRANKIE

TEXAS: *Frozen-custard designer and transgressive artist;* Silk, penne, and potato skin sleeveless "surfer" shirt, $13,400. At Jacques LeBingo. FESTIS BENEDICTI: *Illustrator and underwear collector;* Steel-blend knit top with attached polystyrene tie, $410, by Popp Flikk. At Popp Flikk-Rafe Schnorrer. MOSS ROSES: *Hamburger cuisinier and guitar admirer;* Extruded fudge and linen polo shirt, $995. At Suck-Egg Mule. KIDWELL MAINWARING: *Toilet detailer and loft appraiser;* Cellophane sneakers, $550. At Heroickal Feets. MOZART DELANEY: *Duck-blind furnisher and apple polisher;* "Ham on rye" suit, $3,495 and aluminum-and-synthetic-hemp shirt, $650. Both from I.C. Assappe. At I.C. Assappe. JACK MELBA: *Pet artist;* Snap-front rotted denim jacket, $1,025 and urine-stained jeans, $674. Both from Jason Basura. At Jason Basura. ROBERT RINGLING: *Publishing enthusiast and computer magazine buyer;* Lemon-rind boots from So What? Cobblery, $2,750 and crimped stretch-porcelain sweater jacket, $4,000, from Zeppole. Both at Bygge Deele. SAMUEL URGENTE: *Crayola artist;* Zip-front "knish" jacket, $11,050. At Coney Island Mike's. JINKS MIKADO: *Slang collector and recipe verifier;* Five-button tortured polyvinyl and "wet" swansdown jacket, $16,300. At Sabrett and Nathan.

[Photographed entirely in the Cordillera Mountains and in Jake's Loma Prieta Bar-Bee-Kew, Shots and Beers, Day-Glo Bed-and-Breakfast, Hitler's Place, and the Luxe-on-Luxe Inn. *Photographs by* BILLEE TUESDAY, HELMUT DIMME-BLANCO, and STEPAN BONGO.]

EASTERN SEA

A Time Capsule

Here is a tin pig, sporting a blue, badly painted-on sailor jacket and beating a tin drum; he is laden with dead hopes and wet with useless tears; his imbecile grin goes well with the grey Christmas morning; here is a tin pig with a key in his back; and here a dark booth in a Brooklyn saloon, and the angels sing; in a Bronx saloon, let it snow, let it snow; in a Manhattan saloon, winter wonderland and dark eyes, the wind off the East River knifing its way through the dead, brittle park; a dark booth, a dark night, a beer garden with colored lights swaying and the smell of salt from the bay, sound of foghorns and faint bells from the distant buoys; a snap-brim fedora, pearl grey; a flagstone patio and ice-cold outdoor showers in hot sun; vacant lot; clothes from Carson Pirie Scott, Lincoln Road, Phil Kronfeld, pulled from their exquisite boxes with sour, grudging acceptance, spoiled, soft, rich, expensive and poisoned and damned; a Bulova watch smashed in the middle of Avenue A; nickel-plated .38 Smith and Wesson revolver in a drawer under silk boxer shorts; slacks from Brooks Brothers, tweed jackets from

Hart Schaffner and Marx, lighters by Dunhill, cursed, cursed, and, by Christ, cursed again; vacant lot; the sunlight in vast, smoky bars slathering the floor of Penn Station, all aboard for Miami Beach; a navy dress with white polka dots, white heels, white crocheted gloves, sad face; a Manhattan, a Martini, a Jack Rose, a Clover Club, a Whiskey Sour, a Sazerac, a Sidecar, whiskey, whiskey, gin, rum, quiet laughter at the bar, the snow beginning to fall, and nobody ceaselessly drunk will ever die; bitter cold, concrete platforms piled with freight bound for Jersey, painfully cold wind off the North River, smell of blood and death from the slaughterhouses, a pint of Carstairs for succor; dark eyes; vacant lot; New Year's Eve hotel room, snow falling past the windows into the Brooklyn Heights streets, poor butterfly, she smiles through her tears; bottle of Worcestershire on the blue-and-white-checked tablecloth, bowl of salad, platter of broken heart and acid soul; the old witch in the cellar swigging from a jug of warm Manhattans, the stupid girl; beautiful scarves from John David, silk and cashmere; bewildered face in the mirror, no one will ever die; vacant lot; strong tanned legs and dazzling white shorts; the taste of scotch on Christmas Eve, smoky neighborhood bar, the usual Christmas tunes on the jukebox; orange dress, scent of Conte Castile and subtle flowers exotic in a strange apartment, a white brassiere on a copy of *Life,* hello young lovers, goodbye young lovers, take it easy young lovers, wise up young lovers; Dear John I'll send your saddle home, you dumb fuck, with mixed emotions; letter read and folded, read and folded, read and folded, oh *fuck* her!; a bag of old pots and pans, pitiful; soft mounting roar in the thin clear October sunlight of Ebbets Field; Cadillac Fleetwood limousine and English Ovals and shadow-striped gabardine suits and Borsalino hats and a gold Dunhill; vacant lot; dark lake shining in moonlight; dark pubic hair in a perfect V; moonlight perfume, distant tenors, "Miss Thing"; a chocolate-brown wool worsted suit, black onyx teardrop earrings; the hush before the band thrillingly attacks "Ice Freezes Red," the hush before the tenor edges into the first notes of "Three Little Words," these are men, men!; a martini, and another martini, and yes another martini, and another goddamn fucking martini, the breakfast of champions!; drunken face in the mirror, pale and sickly, ginger snaps and Four Roses will do it every time, fuckhead; clams on the half-shell, a beer garden, sad foghorns from the Narrows, sad?, colored lights and the taste of the sea; a dead woman; a dead man; another dead woman, the smell of corruption beneath the thick scent of flowers; vacant lot; dark pubic V; a dead turkey in the sink, a crate of grapefruit in the bathtub; sixty grand lost on ten the hard way, easy come; Jimmy Gent off at 8 to 5 at Hialeah, running in the mud and out of the money, easy go; pizzaiola, white clam sauce, cannoli, sfogliatelle, and a t'ick minestrone; many, oh many a teardrop may fall; ice frozen red, granita like razzberry, right?; "Ko-Ko"; a bottle of Thunderbird, of Gypsy Rose, some Dexedrine, some Benzedrine, sweltering in Queens, the Bird on ice, you bet your ass, dead as a doornail, as hell, as shit, it's all in the game, it's life; faded khaki shirt, red deuce, Pfc stripes, faded khaki pants; a porch in Flatbush; the Fifth Symphony and

Bullmoose Jackson, the "Jupiter" and Savannah Churchill, time out for tears; Camels and Lucky Strikes; oh, pregnant girl with trembling lip, whosoever fucketh you hath done took a powder; the Ninth Symphony; a bowlegged woman, that's all!; sunlight on the empty beach, sails on the Sound, tight black bathing suit, cool cottage under trees, love, your magic spell is everywhere; Herbert Tareytons, grey Persian lamb, diaphanous white scarf, white tablecloths, and bread sticks; a pack of Chelseas, Virginia Rounds, Twenty Grands, Sweet Caporals, and Wings; old man falling off a chair toward good old Death, patiently waiting, faithful forever, and, oh yes, a hard worker, the roof scenically behind him as he falls, the tar gleaming stickily in the hot spring sun; a tin pig, a woman in brassiere and step-ins, silk stockings and tears, afraid to, afraid to what?; vacant lot; it's all in the game; and strangers, unfamiliar women, weeping bitterly at the casket; flowers, flowers, the flowers.

ERATOSTHENES

Eratosthenes, one of the prize students of Callimachus, was the head of the famed library of Alexandria from about 240 BC till his death in 195 of a surfeit of new wine and adolescent boys. Or so they say. While at the library, and in moments stolen from the cataloguing and repairing of its treasures, Eratosthenes drew a map of the world, working from memory, hearsay, dreams, and the tales of Phoenician sailors. The map on display here at the Rufus X. Noogie Museum of Purest Jade is thought to be Eratosthenes' original. Under its triple layer of shatterproof glass, surrounded by armed guards, and protected by electronic alarms of an almost frightening complexity and efficiency, it sits in its aura of splendid uniqueness. It is generally conceded that were it to be offered for sale at auction, the map, which is only 4 1/2 by 3 1/4 inches in size, would bring in excess of a billion and a half dollars. It is, incidentally, badly drawn, of muddy, indeterminate colors, rife with misspellings, and even for its time, *all wrong*.

FRA MAURO

Our Neighbors, the Italians: Myth and Reality

Happy Tony, whose grandfather was deeply respected by all for helping to build the New York City subway system.

Warm Sal, who stuck a fuckin' ice pick into warm Vito.

Familiar Carmine, who cursed out a Puerto Rican mother, hey, why not, they breed like animals.

Brutal Biaggio, who makes homemade *a pizz'* in his homemade oven in his homemade backyard with the fig trees.

Treacherous Cesare, who bounces his fat, curly-haired babies on his knee, all eighteen of them.

Loud Angie, who cries like a baby when his Mama sings "Sorrento."

Blithe Nino, working ninety hours a week onna garbage truck to send his nephew to Fordham.

Affectionate Sal, he looks like a fuckin' priest, God forgive me, who beat some chooch with a schlammer.

Domestic Rocco, who fucks every broad who'll stand fuckin' still.

Abusive Julie, weeping at his daughter, Yolanda's, First Holy Communion, she was like an angel.

Crafty Tommy, corrupting an entire honest union *all by himself*.

Blatant Patsy, who don't give a shit about his neighbor's rights, fuck them with their barbecues.

Carefree Luigi, who shovels raw garlic by the handful into his laughing mouth.

Amiable Sally, crazy with admiration for all blondes.

Beastly Ray, a connoisseur of loud clothes.

Designing Joey, holding up a fuckin' Jew basted store or maybe he was a fuckin' Armenian.

Cheerful Mooks, who corrupted a virtuous brokerage house on virtuous Wall Street.

Benign Giannino, who once read a book for fun.

Bloodthirsty Curzio, who loves his *pasta e cicc'* like when he was a kid.

Dangerous Donnie Peps, who has like an altar to Joe DiMaggio and Frank Sinatra behind his fruit store.

Garish Richie, who has a mouth he shoulda gone to law school.

Exuberant Frankie Hips, who don't mind moolanyans if they mind their fuckin' business.

Cordial Lou, who smacks his wife, Filomena, on the sconce when she makes the gravy too thin like American fuckin' gravy.

Cold-blooded Artie the Crip, who cries like a broad when he hears Dean Martin sing in Italian it's so beautiful.

Devious Billy Beebee, whose suits and silk shirts all fell off a truck, right?

Noisy Nick Noise, who likes to look for trouble with the niggers in Coney Island.

Gay Choochie, who lost his fuckin' gun in the Fabian Fox balcony one night, the second fuckin' time.

Emotional Nunzio, who makes his own wine like a genius.

Cruel Benny Jinx, who makes out like he's a spic and sells cocaine to the kids in the schoolyard.

Dishonest Gus, who is connected, along with every other Italian in New York, they won't admit it but.

Obstreperous Tonino, who got thrown outta school for leaning on some momo football player fag.

Glad Gino, whose pizza joint is a hangout for all the wise guys in Bath Beach.

Fond Scoogie, who got mad as a bitch 'cause he couldn't get a pepper-and-egg sangwich at the New York Book Fair, which he thought was a feast.

Cutthroat Frankie Fats, who has a fat happy wife and eight fat happy kids, God bless them.

Insincere Gaetano, whose Uncle Pooch practically invented Roosevelt Raceway.

Pushy Rico, who busted some guy's head for sayin' shit about the Virgin Mary, hey!

Gleeful Franco, who told some asshole cop to get the fuck off his Cadillac.

Friendly Jimmy Shots, who is not a bad guy for being half-fuckin' Irish.

Deadly Jackie Buds, who covered his finished basement walls with beautyful maroon and gold woddayacallit, velveteen?

Lying Baby Rufino, who stuck up what turned out to be his *compare*'s gas station over in Elizabeth.

Raucous Patsy Cheech, who was a nice fast middleweight till he got fucked up with a Jewish broad.

Joyful Whitey Bromo, who could play fuckin' Hearts for a year and never win a hand.

Genial Beppo, who ate fifteen calzones at the St. Rocco's feast.

Ferocious Black Sally, who cut some mook's nose off in Sunnyside, don't ask.

Perfidious Jimmy Trey, who took a little of the vig off the top as a regular thing, who they found shot fulla holes on Neptune Avenue.

Rowdy Tommaso, who worked strictly as a union bricklayer 'cause of an oath he took to his mother, God rest her soul.

Merry Clemenza, whose marinara that he put scotch in, was famous even in Naples, no shit.

Good-natured Jackie the Pipe, who says he can get Armanis for like a yard apiece, Armani his ass.

Fierce Papa Gigio, who kissed the ground his wife of forty-six years walked on, Rose.

Scheming Tony Candy, who says he heard that they don't put no tomatoes or mozzarell' in Domino's pizza that tastes like fuckin' shit.

Strident Jerry the Barber, whose three daughters, Robin, Erin, and Tiffany, all married American boys who went to college and don't know the difference between a *cassata* and a *lupara*.

Radiant Googie the Jump, whose sister went to the convent after that rat basted Polack George fuckin' something left her high and dry which was good news for the emergency room, right?

Neighborly Nuzz', whose little candy store on Eighteenth Avenue clears maybe 300 grand a year, God bless him.

Merciless Mario, whose wife of eighteen years still looks, *madonn'*, like the gorgeous chorus girl he married, even though she's not even Italian.

Shifty Nicky Chicago, who always wears porkpie hats like some kind of a *cetrul'* black guy.

Tasteless Corrado, who never picked a horse right in his whole miserable fuckin' life.

Sunny Ralphie, who drives nothing but Cadillacs, fuck you with the German cars, he says.

Sociable Tommy Mouse, who they don't let into Atlantic City even to take a piss anymore.

Murderous Enzo, who says he never knew the guys who got popped over on Ralph Avenue, what balls.

Unscrupulous Harry the Painter, who lets his wife buy anything she wants in Miami Beach, which she says is full of nothing but spics from Cuba over there nowadays.

MORE PHOTOGRAPHS OF THESE IRREPRESSIBLE AND HARD-WORKING AMERICANS, WHO HAVE HELPED TO BUILD OUR GREAT NATION, OR SO THEY SAY, ON THE SECOND FLOOR, REAR GALLERY.

GASSENDI

Banville Teddie: Late Works

This small, exquisitely mounted exhibition shows works from the Gassendi Foundation's collection of Teddie's last miniatures. It is provocatively, if somewhat inaccurately presented under the title "In the Months of Love," a phrase from the juvenilia of Ingelow MacGonagall, a Scottish poet much admired by Teddie, and comprises a group of late paintings from the mysterious "Primavera" series. They are hopefully dreamy, their microscopically gestural bravura "in love," so to say, with the notion of ideal beauty, their colors almost vengefully Parnassian. And yet, this dreaminess is quite proper, perhaps, to aesthetes, while not yet quite so to poets, to whom, *en masse*—as we know from Teddie's recently discovered diaries—these delicate miniatures were dedicated, and for whom they were most certainly executed. This dreamy quality of Teddie's work is often thought of as a flaw, and yet one cannot remotely conceive of the paintings otherwise. Teddie increasingly thought of himself as a poet, and of his colors as words, his forms, as he once put it, "[as] a shifting syntax, of sorts," and his canvases as his "well-thumbed, scratched over, blotted" manuscripts, all brushed by the hand of the Muse, "yet no *more* than her hand, no more, no more." The canvases, one must declare, are much smaller, even, than miniatures, and are each dominated by a cool, sherbet-like color, although other colors, tints, shades, tones, and highlights, lurk everywhere. These are, perhaps, after all, "the months of love." Perhaps not. The pictures, so small as to be made out with no little difficulty, are madly ambitious, a kind of paean to a strange Teddiean spring, to his beloved primavera, and to the sun, the sun of the artist's cherished Ringo Chingado Flats, the site of his last isolated studio; and, of course, to flesh, the flesh of his fellow humans, mostly women, that he honored and adored, even as he exploited, brutalized, and despised it.

GRIMALDI

In an unprecedented outpouring of affection and respect for Anastasia Humboldt-Grimaldi's championing of risky art, her trenchant yet unfailingly generous critical writing, and her unwavering support of contemporary exhibit spaces, the Dimension Matrix Galerie (recently relocated in the basement of the newly Re-Reformed Gospel New Disciples Church of Self-Love in Bayside, Queens) presented a one-night vernissage of new works by thirty-four of today's most highly acclaimed new artists. All of the works, including "Heinz Beppo's Marsalis Dream," by McClark Lott, an installation especially erected for Ms. Humboldt-Grimaldi, are dedicated to her on the occasion of her retirement as chief art-and-cinema critic for *Ici*. Yet just who is Anastasia Humboldt-Grimaldi? Is she every man's girlfriend, the girlfriend of the whirling dervish, the girl from Ipanema, the girl in expensive tights, the girl that somebody left behind, the "shadow dance" girl, the girl that somebody loved in sunny Tennessee, the girl in the Alice blue gown, the girl in the crinoline gown, the girl with the big thing in her, the girl of the Moravian peasant factory, the girl who proudly blows the trumpet, the girl who is you, the girl who is like you, the girl who is like another girl, the girl of somebody's feverish dreams, the girl who is an occasion of sin, the girl of Pi Beta Phi, the girl on the magazine cover, the girl who paid $84 for a T-shirt, the girl on *Happening!,* the girl who was compromised in the stock room, the girl that somebody marries, the girl that somebody wants to marry, the girl in the closet, the girl with a brogue, the girl with the golden braids, the girl who threw up at a party for a famous person, the girl who was the sweetheart of the whole battalion, the girl whom lust made free, the girl who rewrote the "Dear John" letter, the girl with the fake Rolex watch, the girl for whom "it" is not about money, the girl who eats and eats, or—is she simply WOMAN? Whatever she is, was, or will be in the exciting aesthetic future, she's still got terrific legs, and the edgy and vibrant art world would agree with Jefty Vogel's characterization of Ms. Humoldt-Grimaldi as "a round-tripper homer slugger like Kent Griffin [*sic*]."

HUMBOLDT

Arrttbbeatt Chelsea

The first chalice holds a glorious naked girl, perfect in all ways, gentle, beautifully proportioned, and, as the artist's notes inform us, "modest in public and lascivious beyond telling" at home. The small room is dark and the only sounds audible are those from the vintage Wurlitzer juke-box that plays "And the Angels Sing" repeatedly. The moon looks down, the night grows deep, the sky over the bay turns a profound black as the moon "takes a powder." The girl may well be locked into her own personally invented and meticulously nourished misery, and soon enough. The second chalice holds nothing, as do the third and fourth chalices. These are not true chalices, but grape-jelly jars, although this matters little, since "this" is not about money! A hat rack completes the installation. When queried, the artist, Benjie Kooba, whose "Semen Dreamin'" piece at the Smith Street Atelier last spring was criticized by the Purity Commission as the cause of wholesale nocturnal impropri-eties among morally susceptible citizens, remarks: "Don't ask *me!*" He is wearing loose-fitting trousers of unbleached linen, well-worn sandals, and a black T-shirt, the very picture of the hot young artist. He is just *adorable*, despite his snaggle tooth and things.

HYGINUS RILLE

The annual Groundbreakers exhibit consists primarily of the "Effete," as the useful if not especially knowledgeable catalogue insists on calling the various imagings that comprise this year's show. Debbie Danfort, the curator of the exhibition, is, not to put too fine a point on it, a "dumb broad," as they say in the meatpacking district's hippest and hottest diners, even though she occasionally reviews—you'll pardon the expression—new fiction, whatever that may be, for *The New York Times Book Review*. In any event, this year we have wild maladies of the sky, green shades, the radiance, the radiance, the stars' bliss in blissful heaven, seasons in the evening, and a green beast, a bloated beast, a beast serene in the purple shade of a copse called "Satan's Ear," and a sleepy, mildewed, fat beast to, as they like to say, boot; then there is a startling display of summer, broiling, humid, stinking, rotting, with its moisture, its heat, its sticky sidewalks, madness, crime, murder, lust, and noise, rank blooms, sagging trees, overgrown gardens, tough jays and dusty grackles and boss crows, the sweet virtuosic repertoire of grey mockingbirds on the evening air, from black trees, from rose skies, from beyond the blue hydrangeas, next to which stands an authentic honest-to-God young virgin in white linen dress, white stockings, white shoes, her hair tied back in a chignon with a white silk ribbon, it's too good to be true, her hand extended toward one of the massive nodding blooms. All this has been managed so as to arouse the brittle laughter of the cruel, the stupid, the shambling half-dead in putrefyingly expensive clothes; whose seams gap and tear; whose seams pop open or rip immediately upon wearing; "who may die before their time, *Deo volente,*" some bitter and unpleasant person says on an elevator.

J. HERSCHEL

Visions of a Visionary: J. Herschel and His Times
Photographs and Memorabilia from the J. Herschel Collection

J. Herschel with a letter to his mother; J. Herschel with a bouquet of moss roses; J. Herschel where his love lies dreaming; J. Herschel and the fifth Mrs. Herschel having their "morning ride" at Rancho Seymour; J. Herschel posing with a letter from his mother; J. Herschel and Harry Norman pore over Norman's collection of musical gems; J. Herschel in pursuit of the young ladies of the Slocum Musical Society; J. Herschel arguing for "social restraint" in the well of the House of Representatives; J. Herschel playing a bunting horn; J. Herschel and an unidentified woman in the bath; J. Herschel throwing nickels and dimes to a group of freshly washed homeless people; J. Herschel studying one of his 412 dubious Picassos; J. Herschel playing "Jealousy" on an electrified accordion; J. Herschel beating out some hot jive on a fourteen-karat gold tambourine; J. Herschel playing with himself and others at Ascot; J. Herschel under the piano with a young maid dressed in his fourth wife's clothes; J. Herschel giving his celebrated talk, "Let's Read a Lot," to members of the Stanford University

English Department; J. Herschel and Mr. Carney Grain dressed as Sisters of Charity; J. Herschel and the "mighty drum major," Julian Scott, enjoying a few Super Bowl heroes; J. Herschel lunching on nuts and weeds at the Wallace Stegner Foothills Cottage; J. Herschel dressed as Doctor Music; J. Herschel claiming that some of his best friends are Jews; J. Herschel on a quiet evening in the library with Reinhard Heydrich's souvenir photo album, "Poland"; J. Herschel abusing himself to the point of madness to photos of Jenny Lind in her corsets; J. Herschel and Mabel A. Royds, the "choir boy"; J. Herschel at the Grand Opening of Cleveland's Blackamoor Minstrels in Washington, D.C.; J. Herschel and the Reverend Branford Christy, the devout embezzler, chuckling at the Rolling Stones lying in vomit; J. Herschel and Mrs. Christy doing something for which there is no name on the beach at Rio; J. Herschel with the original "lost" draft of Gilbert and Sullivan's shocking joint confession; J. Herschel inventing the computer program, PanUrge; J. Herschel and the Bohemian Club of San Francisco making water amid the majestic redwoods; J. Herschel buying Southward Fair; J. Herschel buying the Prado; J. Herschel buying Topeka, Kansas; J. Herschel fainting at the beauty and charm of the fine restaurants of Palo Alto, California, "where dining is a skill"; J. Herschel masquerading as Albert Speer on the last day of Oktoberfest; J. Herschel demonstrating the correct way to eat spaghetti to the ignorant Neapolitans; J. Herschel and Louise Bathy, "Venus's contortionist," eating soup off each other's heads; J. Herschel getting an injection of penicillin for what he often called "the old Joe"; J. Herschel somberly displaying the toilet seat that infected him with the AIDS virus; J. Herschel dancing the rhubarb dance with Moravian peasants in his "return to my roots" excursion; J. Herschel lecturing on the errors made by Captain Cook on his ninth voyage to Sandy Hook; J. Herschel in his Female Blondin costume; J. Herschel cavorting with Mrs. Grandwill and her Company of Sluts; J. Herschel with some of his best friends, none of whom *look* Jewish; J. Herschel finding God and peace and serenity and regretting his ruthless, selfish, corrupt life; J. Herschel screaming as he is whisked to hell by three demons, all of whom seem pleased with the assignment, jaded though they may be.

JOLIOT-CURIE

In letters of purest jade: MY LINGERIE IS WORTH MORE THAN YOUR CAR; of shocking pink neon: WOMAN, WOOGIE OR BOOGIE?; of rarest lapis lazuli: ART IS GOOD BUSINESS; of pale bauxite: THERE ARE NO MASTERPIECES; of matte beryllium: I SMELL LIKE A DOITY SKOIT; of Hungarian chalcedony: BIG LOFTS ARE BIG FUN; of scarlet aluminum: DON'T CELEBRATE YESTERDAY; of rhinestone bakelite: CHE BABA CHE BABA CHE BABA; of salsified pearlite: FUCK EL GRECO; of lodestone ebony: MEN ARE PISSERS. Barbrah Joliot-Curie's conflicting and intrusive MESSAGES, all of which tend toward the metaphysical noise that may be termed the emblematic substitute for what was once mistakenly valorized as a value-based system of so-called "high art," implicate and suggest a complex, actually, of shifting signs, arranged so as to transgressively subvert modes of corporate anti-colonialist, pre-magicorealist inscription. This gesture is never enough to make one embrace the rebarbative, as Benjamin implies, and rush, metaphorically, to Dom's Heroes for one of his famous "hoagies," and yet it is *almost* enough. In point of fact, Dom's

Extra-Special Hoagie may be culturally indexed as an authentic work of petit-bourgeois, working-class art, and, as such, asserts itself as a proletarian icon whose task it is to displace the various capitalist icons of nonrepresentational complicity. "Hoagies, A Meal in Itself," as Dom's shrewdly hand-lettered sign states—the grammatical paradigm carefully distorted so as to render the normative plural singular—boldly insists on the labile, collapsing the symbolic into nothing more than an aporia. And the naïve injunction, EAT MY SANDWICHES, IT'S DELICIOUS!, in glossy black on white cardboard, becomes, then, a radically salutary act of cultural infringement.

JULES VERNE

A cluster (bunch) of disparate items (things) some of them words, and nothing else but words, HUDDLE(s) in the corner LIKE smokers outside a building. So crack (expert) JOURNALISTS often (more times than you can shake a stick at) WRITE. The things (items) pretend to be art, but they are, essentially, a bunch (cluster) of shit (crap). "We'll see about that!" one thing (smoker) notes, apparently from among (amid) the disparate items (buildings), for all (everybody else) to see.

Jules Verne, *Les aventures du Capitaine Maison*, 1864

JURA MOUNTAINS

A staggered pile, something like a perverted, tortured ziggurat in shape, of fawn-colored bricks, many bricks, much too many to be counted, sprawls across the floor of the Kansas Jura Gallery. The whole is transgressive of something, even subversive, but of what? The piece might be a static representation of an early Stones tune married, gloriously, with a "drone-and-squeal" sound project by the Lombardo Collaborative. The bricks, in their essential posture of gestural, defiant decrepitude, manifest a core transgressive spirit (if "spirit" is not too grandiose a word, and if Jamón is to be given any credence, it is not), one that is rigorously detached from the paradigmatic pieties of the fading Zeitgeist and the late phallo-millennium. The occasional fly that settles on the bricks serves to recall their primary significatory duties, as if these everyday *objets* are, indeed, no more than horseshit, even though that may be their *nominative* potential, rather than their constative one. In any event, as signifiers, they gesture toward the salutary emptiness that one discovers in the spaces of a poem by Mallarmé, and never in the words themselves. It is, then, Mallarmé to whom we must turn in order to permit this haunting, oddly rhomboidal construct to assert its cone-like, cubist, empty qualities, qualities which are, at once, always terrible, absent, yet eerily sublime, and, perhaps most movingly, qualities that insist on the absence that is within the implied absence of the brick pile itself. The sun which slants in through the quite perfectly grimy skylight touches the work with the poignancy of nature forgotten if not nature betrayed, nature ignored if not nature assaulted. The silent and somehow disheveled construct seems to emerge, at such times, from the very earth itself, and its stillness is that of the greatest, or, at least, the pleasantly mediocre, works of art.

LAKE OF DREAMS

Film Loop

A man talks to a woman who turns out to be his wife, since she has always been his wife, although, at present, she is slightly different, or perhaps it is that she was slightly different in the past. She is wearing the grey, fitted suit that he has always liked, black patent leather pumps, and sheer, off-black nylon stockings. The drinks at the bar, for they are in a dim and quiet cocktail lounge, which await the man and his beautifully dressed wife, for she is, he admits, his wife, are on a tray, and yet no waiter is present; for that matter, no barman is in sight. Charles seems to be his name, or so he said. The drinks are four—two in champagne flutes and two in cocktail glasses. Those in the champagne flutes are of the palest steel blue, a blue so utterly pale that it verges on the colorless; it is the color which gave to gin the beautiful name, *blue ruin*. Those drinks in the cocktail glasses are cerulean blue, the blue of Apollinaire's fake Texas skies. He calmly says, "Blue ruin is a beautiful name," and looks down at the cocktail lounge from a stingily appointed office, one of whose walls is glass from floor to ceiling. It is through this glass wall that he looks to see his wife, now sitting at a different table, and dressed in a navy blue suit, her legs crossed so that her thighs are discreetly yet provocatively exposed. "Your skirt," he says to her, but she cannot hear him, of course. Who is the relentless person behind him, who is talking, talking, talking to him as he tries to think of a way back to the cocktail lounge, to the woman who is his wife, to the glamorous and unearthly drinks, to his youth and her young womanhood? To scotch and the clean whiteness of their belated wedding day, lovely and dreamily out of focus? Who, for Christ's sake, *is* this motherfucking bastard? Some homeless lout who should have died in the gutter yesterday? The man who speaks gibberish from out of the moon? Some kind of mastermind?

LANGRENUS

What, precisely, was it about Claude Langrenus, often called
the King of Transgression, the Broom King, the Emperor of
Mustard, Royal Claudie, and, most usually, simply the King,
that prompted so many distinguished photographers of the
San Francisco Bay Area to take, conservatively speaking, thousands upon thousands of photographs of Kingorooney, as he
was known to many, photographs of him in the performance
of everyday tasks, tasks that one might think too trivial to
occupy, even for a moment, the King of Ideas and Theatre, as
he was occasionally dubbed? The "scholarship of the image," to
which we owe so much, has collectively determined that
there are presumed to be, roughly, some 43,976 images of
Lord Faucet, as he was known to close friends, and, remarkably, that those images represent the King of Canned
Tomatoes, as that legendary figure was called by the beloved
street urchins of San Francisco, city of fogs and food, of hills
and highways, of crystal air and cable cars, of art, art, and ever
more art; and that the "tomato monarch" may well be
Langrenus himself, shown in a number of mundane activities

and things that appeal to the sophisticated citizens of "Kansas
on the Bay," as The City is known to its oldest residents, some
of whom were last seen in Noe Valley looking for signs of life
on the quiet streets. Langrenus, or the King of Tomatoes, or
"Larry," is seen admiring an organ grinder's monkey, and, in
a few cases, an organ grinder; running in terror from a bear
who is attacking a youthful companion; laughingly strapping
on a "lady's helper"; being cheated by a three-card monte
dealer while he smirks the smirk of chumps everywhere;
fleeing in panic from a Pekingese who is chewing on an old
woman's knee; buying a deluxe edition of *Théâtre Epinal* by
"Chet"; pissing up a rope. Just who *was* Claude Langrenus?
Prize-winning chemist, multimillionaire inventor, hack nov-
elist, wretched playwright, furniture designer, fashion plate,
and much-loved lecturer on the horror of phallocentrism in
the rest room, yes, yet happy to be thought of as, simply,
King Corn Flakes. These remarkable photographs, a mere
sampling of the rich treasures stored in the vaults of the
California Palace of the Legion of Honor Annex, will not tell
us. Sadly, the King of Oxycetabutylinase, as he was teasingly
called by the hobos, rakes, and ladies of the evening of
Russian Hill, remains a mystery to all—still *another* mystery
shrouded in the fogs and mists of the brooding Bay Area that
many call home!

LONGOMONTANUS

Corporal Wing is chopping celery in the company mess and in the meantime Chinese mortars are laying down elegant patterns of death with lazy, terrible precision, the gooks, as they are called on this wall placard (hereon "Gooks"), can put a fucking round right up your ass if you're unfortunate enough to bend over. It's an inspiring collage, now you see him, now you see him as little chunks of seared flesh and splintered bone whizzing through the air. In full color. One magazine, ball ammunition, lock and load. And setting off the stirring photos of soldiers going about their everyday business is a wonderfully *honest* shot of Second Lieutenant Arthur M. Codgille crisply saluting the First Sergeant, Robert Swanson, with his left hand, it's adorable, the picture nicely set off with a border of OCS patches. A comic-strip balloon, in, as someone once mysteriously said, "lonely majesty," contains a message, to wit: THEY TOLD US WE WAS EE-FECTING A STRATEGIC WITHDRAWL, BUT ACKSHULLY WE WAS FLEEING IN WILD DISORDER. And here's an authentic mess hall sign: Salusbury steak au juice, mash potatos, string beans, apple sause, mix salad, bread and butter, milk, coffee, ice cream. Ready on the right. Take all you want, you pussies. Ready on the left. Eat all you take, you cunts. And here is what seems to be a deposition by one Corporal John Roy Whitfield, Infantry, an astigmatic and slow-witted machine-gunner. Ready on the firing line. Corporal Whitfield's complaint stipulates that various (and numerous) members of his platoon pissed on him throughout a long night during which he slept drunkenly in the urinal trough of the second platoon's barracks latrine. The flag is up. No fucking *way*. The flag is waving. To treat a fucking noncommissioned officer. The flag is down. In the fucking United States Army. Commence firing. And a swell line drawing, delicate as all get out, left as a farewell note by a man whom the hogs ate soon after he went to shit, a diagram, actually, of how to string empty beer cans, each containing a few pebbles, on concertina wire. The whimsical caption reads: "When the clinkety-clink of the pebbles against the interiors of the cans is heard by the alert gunners, they can fire with the reasonable assurance that they are going to blow apart any fucking gook unlucky enough to be part of an initial assault, oh yes." Stand at ease, soldier! How long have you been *in* the Army? The walls are brilliantly yet soberly painted in shades of khaki and olive drab.

[EXHIBITION CONTINUES ON SECOND FLOOR]

MOSCOW SEA

And here at last is Sir Banjo Hyde-Morrissey's private collection of erotica. The titles of the drawings, prints, mezzotints, gouaches, woodcuts, and watercolors on display follow: Bagpipes in the Boudoir; Eating La Musette; The Burgemote Horns and Their Doxies; Presentation of the Giant Champion Bugle to the Young Queen; Blowing the Massive Horns of Westminster; Shock Tactics and French Ticklers; The Depraved Trumpeter at St. Anne's Nunnery; Lifelong Companions, or, Asshole Chums; Queers at Table, with Gewgaws; Warriors Blushingly Confess; Albanian Musician Discovering Yorkshire Pussy; Young Ladies, in Deshabille, Fleeing Albanian Janitors; Serbs Humping Albanian Janitors, or Anybody; African Women Doing Dirty Things with Their Colonialist Oppressors; Burmese Musicians and a Popular Sponge; Apollo, with Harp and Hard-On; David Playing the Harp with Hard-On; Bellhop, with Hard-On and Pears; Woman Gazing at Hard-On in Window; Corinthian Kate in Cellophane Underwear; Harp and Details of Harp, with Hard-On and Apples in Shadow;

Jeune Demoiselle Touchant "La Harpe"; Lady Playing Harpsichord, with Self-Abusing Boy in Doorway, and Daffodils; Politician with Organ-Grinder's Monkey, with Banana, in Naples; An Increasing Nuisance Concerning a Lady's Privates; A Band of Savoyards at Orgy, with Stuffed Kestrel; College Professors Liven Up Another Meeting, with Scattered Papers; University Don with Old Lecture Notes and Hard-On; Grotesque Scenes of Deviltry with Monkeys, on Windy Moor; Norwegian Lutherans Disrobe After Barn-Raising, with Lutefisk and Lingonberries; The Celebrated American Pianist, Bellowman, Mounting His Steinway, with Peaches and Onions; Mother and Dad Beneath the Chifferobe; Violin Hump; Lady Mary Campbell Tries a "Rubbing" with Dr. Joseph Hollman, the Old Viennese Prongmaster; Dr. Joseph Hollman Fiddles While Lady Campbell Pollutes Herself; Dr. Hollman Dons Lady Campbell's Intimate Garments, with Zucchini; The Garden Fairy Orchestra of Canterbury Tuning Their Dildoes; Dildoes in Action, with Quince and Rutabaga; Lady Mary Campbell Brings Joy to the Garden Fairy Orchestra; Hungarians Frigging Dr. Joseph Hollman, in Legumes and Forage Crops; Hungarians Frigging Lady Mary Campbell; Hungarians Mounting Borrowed Lutefisk; African Women, with Pears and Hungarians; Albanian Janitor with Head Under Corinthian Kate's Skirts; The Boys of St. Bart's and Lady Mary Campbell Playing "Lost in the Gorse"; Old Waitresses in Love with Grotesque Monkeys; Waitress with Ass in Skillet; The Chef Examines His All-Girl Staff; Lady Diner Admiring Sommelier's Tight Trousers; Diner with

Hard-On Sampling Ferret Paté; Young Woman Smiling at Filthy Thought; College Professors Touching Thighs on Dais, with Name Tags and Bow Ties; Woman in Kitchen Watching Monkey Humping Casserole; Leather Madness Bewitches Waitress; Romberg's Symphony Orchestra in Carnal Frenzy, with Toys and Language Poetry Manifesto; Lady Mary Campbell and Her Vibrating Oboe; SS Einsatzgruppenführer Discovering Louisville Slugger in Rectum; Quartet Party in Nude Frolic on Lawn, with Dried Leaves and Canned Peas; Henry Norman Surprised Anew in the Boys' Room; The Famous Vienna Lady Orchestra Let Themselves Go; A Morning Ride, or, Unnatural Congress Between Lady Julia Pemberton and Her Stallion, "Lucifer"; Jenny Lind and Max, the Polish Tenor, with Charlotte Russe, Gourd, and Corsets; Miss Lind in the Puttit Inn Motel, with Ham on Rye; Madame Nellie Melba and Father Dirk Scucciamenza Between the Pews; North Dakotan Monkeys and Lotte Peschjka-Leutner with Her Sister, Candi Brittnee, in Bondage Frolic; A Musical Doctor Alone with a Prized Student's Skirt; The Village Choir at It Again, with Lawn Jockey; Wandering Minstrels with Lutes and Exposed Privates; Mabel A. Royds Corrupting Altar Boys, with Missals; The Delaware Minstrels Discover the Joy and Warmth, Courage and Heartbreak of Gay Life; and, perhaps the most remarkable item, a rare and perfect dry-platinum-and-alum-process linoleum blocking of Cleveland and Billy Hill in their Great Double Song, Dance, and Buggery Act, with Banjos and Trombones, Cricket Bats, and Hand-Colored Daguerrotypes of Lady Edith Tyne-Fforke and Lady

Martha Barley-Headde, Aspiring Pilots Both, Legs Akimbo, Sweating and Moaning Beneath a Perfect Replica of the Tattered Union Jack Flown by Lord Nelson at Trafalgar and the Second Battle of the Nile.

ΠEPER

A legerdemain icon, carefully handcrafted in the ancient and sadly anachronistic "tile mills" of Tynemouth-Bourne-Stetson on Palseyshire, broods, as it were, monochromatically, above the grime-streaked window that looks out on the rain-darkened street below. The difficult configurations of the disconcerting "construction" remind some visitors, paradoxically, of the hand-colored wood engraving of the assassination of Abraham ("Abe") B. Lincoln at Ford's Famous Theater and Emporium (such a realization is invariably chilling, and has made more than one person quite literally sick); still, the "moral intrusiveness," as Michelle Caccatanto has trenchantly put it in one of her dazzling occasional essays on popular culture—which is, as she has noted, "so much *more* than popular culture"—of "La Folie au Monde," the title by which the work is commonly known, has convinced an equal number of viewers to see in it a classic Dutch street fair with traveling stage and performers—the latter joyously akimbo in the whirl of a traditional Dutch Sunday in Neper. Such, then, is the power of the ancient

Tynemouth craftsmen and the products of their time-tested thunking, gathering, carding, wooling, ratcheting, and blooring, made, as they have always been made, in the mist-shrouded valleys of the lower-central-midlands of the verdant Cotswolds and their crystalline lakes, aromatic fens, and glowing heaps of tossed midden, not to mention the acres of dead-grey gorse that say "home!" "La Folie," as it is familiarly known to its many devotees, can be, as Ms. Caccatanto has noted, "many things to many persons," yet it always gently insists on its "grave, brooding humanity" and its "true message" of steadfastness and "courage." A few commentators have suggested that Ms. Caccatanto's deeply respectful essay quietly suggests her hidden sense of herself, in the presence of so immortal an icon as "La Folie," as a deluded purveyor of empty blather, the very picture of the impotent and self-deluded cultural critic; but they, as one of her defenders smilingly remarks, "don't make half her salary." The sunlight, by the by, brings the obscurest recesses of the object to sudden, startling *life*.

OCEAN OF STORMS

A number of large television sets—seven, to be precise—
show, continuously, the same film, variously titled *The Past,
Rock Island Rock,* or *Celebrity Toodle-oo*. Each is played, if that's
the word, at a different speed, if that's the word, so that the
imagery, as well as the narrative, such as it is, in each film is
identical, the differing speeds at which this imagery and narrative are deployed, if that's the word, enforcing the sense or
idea that the viewer, the ideal viewer, is being presented
with seven different films. This is posolutely correct, a construction facilitator notes, using a whimsical coinage, if
that's the word, said to be invented by Joe Penner or Ed
Wynn on the old vaudeville circuit. They, and others, often
played the Palace, nicely named, since playing the Palace was
thought of as making it big, getting the big break, making
the big time, hitting it big, and grabbing the brass ring. Betty
Grable, Alice Faye, Ginger Rogers, Ruby Keeler, and
Jeanette MacDonald all hit the big time and got the big
break in cinematic representations of vaudeville days, those
glorious days that will come no more. Whatever, by God,

happened to the *melted snows?* One of the most famous of the cinematic versions of vaudeville stars' lives and times was played, if that's the word, quite improbably, by Esther Williams, or so they say. Miss Williams, on loan from one of her ocean-liner-Palm Beach-Sun Valley-Rio movies, the latter group nicely augmented by such reliable plodders as Xavier Cugat, José Iturbi, Ethel Smith, and Danny Kaye—not to mention Virginia Mayo, Jane Powell, and Kathryn Grayson and her technicolor bust—was uncommonly fetching, if not flagrantly erotic, in black tights and rhinestone tiara. Her rendition of "Waiting at the Church," in a game albeit pathetic Cockney accent was universally greeted by awed silence. The title of this film, which told, not too courageously, the story of Grace DesMoines, was *Rock Island Waltz.* As intelligence concerning these facts permeates the viewing room, the television sets, one at a time, display, on their glistening blue ponds of screens, snow, and nothing but snow, which is understood by all to be unreal, i.e., it is not *snow* in any way, shape, or form. It is but a manifestation of interference, if that's the word, and its grey, black, and white, nervously mobile horizontal lines remind the viewer of the lost snows of something or other. Say, vaudeville.

PETAVIUS

The New Cincinnati Opera House in New Petavius, Bingo County, presents the citizens of Viejo Laredo, Gulf City of Southern Texas, in a series of tasteful romantic tableaux, staged in a replica of the Grand Ballroom of the Walnut Street Theatre, the last true bastion of Philadelphia's stinking rich. The cast will be ably assisted by the clientele of San Francisco's newly chic Bagel Atelier, each person of which will represent a "humor" or "sight" or "odor," as these are traditionally portrayed on the stages of the fabled Komische Oper in Wien, the Old Bouwerie in New York, and the Oakland Melodeon, previously the Royal Chinese Theater in San Francisco, which wonderful old house slid into the bay during last winter's refreshing rains. The staged reading of "Burning of the Brooklyn Theatre at the Washington Street Entrance," justly admired for its celebration of general priapism among the British aristocracy, will be the coda to the Opera House's first "act"; it will be followed, after a brief intermission for refreshments—among which will be, of course, Ohio's inimitable chocolate-mushroom casserole

bites and autumn straw-juice—by an offering of improvisa-
tional sketches based on themes drawn from "Scenes from
Bismarck, North Dakota," and "Exhalations of the Evening
Sky above the Wall where Marcellus Expired," two compelling scenarios of love, lust, and desire, passion and the
wheat harvest: primeval and undeniable forces that "urge
us," as Captain William Westie wrote so pungently, "to get
one's still-warm ashes hauled but good."

[Photographs, bibelots, postcards, blotters, bricks, posters,
mugs, lanterns, pens, pencils, letter openers, baseball caps,
tents, sweatshirts, and genuine mahogany veneer wall
plaques with gold-leaf trim that bear the likenesses of
Picasso, Virginia Woolf, Barbra Streisand, Rimbaud, Einstein,
and Leonard Bernstein chatting with Woody Allen will be on
sale in the lobby and in selected fine-foods markets throughout Cincinnati, and in midwestern states to be named.]

PLATO

"The enormity of the old tableau's collapse cannot prepare us for that which will happen sometime next month." So reads the entire text. The nicely designed placard informs us of other "things to come" as well, including the imminent arrival of Carter the Great, the World's Weird Wonderful Wizard. The visitors, who may purchase logo ties and sweatshirts, as well as souvenir cups and other items that would seem to be nameless, are *part* of the missing tableau. Words not only make statements, but when tossed about on the page, make more, much more, than mere statements. Observe these words and their potential for scattering. One is tempted to inquire, and be done with it at last, "performance art?" But we will never, it appears, be done with *that*. There is one word in the corner of the placard, just blinking on, with the sense of total aliveness that it may soon have! (Scissors are available at the logo desk.) These words make a statement, of that there can be little doubt; oh, not the usual stale conceptualizations, but the usual stale reconceptualizations, or "the ticket." Two of them, as a matter of fact, are at the far edge of another placard, over *there*. Dislodged from the shackles of the diachronic, if "dislodged" is the word, or, for that matter, *a* word, the letters may be readjusted to suggest, as they are currently being readjusted to suggest, up there near the ceiling, or what we have agreed to call the "ceiling," as the glittering new millennium lurches into being: **1937: GERMANY'S FESTIVAL YEAR**. It's just a little too close, however, to the air duct, to be wholly satisfactory. And yet, and yet: the plain, functional duct seems, quite marvelously, to *be*.

POSIDONIUS

Maximus Valerius Posidonius, all of whose writings have been lost, yet whose theories of solar vital forces and rock-removal as a methodology for the prediction of the movements of large bodies of infantry, prefigured the contemporary strategies concerning the deployment of conscripted troops as assistants of various types in the preparation and serving of food, i.e., hot meals, and the maintenance of dining areas within the larger system of the order of battle, is thought to have conceived the notion of cosmic sympathy, and the employment of certain elements of post-Attic Stoicism, to hoist petards and launch Greek fire, shine Phoenician brass, and find the direction whence come and whither go sunbeams during extended thunderstorms, so as to better answer the questions of often surly travelers, stuffed, even bloated, with pita bread and roast lamb—at that time (ca. 94 BC) the only food available in the vast wastes of a particularly arid Syria (known, at that time, as "the Congo")—is also thought to have taught his students the secrets of grinding eggshells for use as the basic component of a particularly fine spackle, corn flakes, ink, and heroin, secrets improbably locked into number theory and its attentions to the special properties of the integers, e.g.: unique factorization, primes, equations with integer coefficients, (biophantine equations), and congruences; and although earlier thinkers (Galen, Dombrowski, Galento, Fitts-Couggh, Gavilan) laid the groundwork for such discoveries with their invention of algebra, Posidonius's work has about it a certain furtive elegance, an elegance much apparent in the exhibition of his astonishing solar-storm drypoints. The exhibition has, unfortunately, unexpectedly and abruptly closed, and its contents subsequently lost or destroyed.

PTOLEMAEUS

The histrionic and lyric firmament—brilliantly spangled with tinsel stars—hangs above the rose-tinted photo-collage of scenes from the Cincinnati Opera Festival's celebrated production of John Gay's *The Beggar's Opera*. A letter from Jacques Offenbach, attesting to his fondness for Gay's masterpiece, is quite beautifully yet simply framed in gentian eucalyptus, a wood known for its lustrous qualities and astonishing durability. Jenny Lind sang the wood's praises in a lost aria from *I Puritani,* an unjustly neglected operetta by Anna Bolena, performed, for the first and only time, for Henry Ford, Ed Rafferty, and Grover Cleveland Alexander. Scenes from *La Gioconda,* digitally altered to include portrayals of Brünnhilde in unnatural congress with her stallion, Fritz, temper the dazzling (to some almost painfully so) light from the glowing firmament. Although some Christian Fundamentalist visitors are distressed, even appalled, by the activities of the Wagnerian heroine and her beloved charger, others—happily, the great majority—know that art's function is to disturb, to question, to disgust, to bore, to nauseate, to make what General Tod Burlingame, Air Force, Retired, called "the big green." The classic American diner booth, ca. 1949, that asserts its vinyl presence within a shallow alcove at a sudden turning of the wall, is flooded with a penetratingly vulgar orange light, and invites a bittersweet nostalgia in its contrast with the shifting of the erotic tableaux of the *La Gioconda* display. The whole diner "thing" permits one to recall a purer, more innocent era: of Stalingrad, Iwo Jima, Monte Cassino, Tarawa, Dresden, Hiroshima, and, of course, Auschwitz—"the good old days," as they are wistfully called. The refreshments—cheeseburgers, French fries, bow ties, Mae Wests, and weak coffee—that crowd the formica-topped table of the diner booth are marvelously crafted of high-impact plastic, and look quite real. At precisely eighteen minutes past the hour, every hour, the pop hit made famous by Andy Warhol and his "gang," "Bobino Josephine," in the Boston Pops-Carly Simon version, is piped into the room, an aural complement to the "spectacle" of late-night variety show outtakes. Media critics, as well as their highbrow art-critic cousins, characterize the whole presentation as a profound example of "people's art."

PURBACH

New Departures, New Arrivals, Old Masters

The quick wit and twisted imagery of Johnstone Sanderson's "Nancy" poempix; the unexpurgated love letters, chock full of uninhibited and shimmery filth, of Sanderson William; William MacLise's generous doses—several in number—of delirious "steel prose"; MacLise Brown's August ice-cream gouaches, disgustingly compelling; fucking "discourse" and fucking "tropes" and the like, by Brown Forster; the Clitoris Commando Series by the newly notorious, self-styled "Cunt Mama," Forster John; John Charles's frothy bubbles (or froth *and* bubbles) of burgeoning narrative; embedded tautology atop disinterred ontology created *in vacuo* by Charles Angela, the veteran assemblagist; the sheer vivacity, exuberance, and extravagance of Angela Collins's "Sheer" portfolio; Collins Anna's moving photographs of homeless street poets honing their craft; exciting stools of the famous, collected and bronzed by Anna Wilkie of the Atelier de Zotz group; adored meaning, conceived and represented by Wilkie Wendell; Wendell & Warren's Colorado photos of young people thirsty for art and fun; reconstructions in miniature of charming, friendly, and badly stocked neighborhood bookstores, by Lemon Burdette; Burdette Jones's glitzy, edgy objects full of elusive racial overtones; a razzberry from el Bronx by Dawn Wasserman's Gun Hill Road Gang of Gay Girls; Brooklyn boogie, boogie woogie, and woogie wonderland, created by Wasserman Harrison Associates; Harrison Blacke's little church upon the corner; a cluster of symbolic pens by Blacke White; breathtaking plot-divagation charts, in twenty colors, by White Thorne; distant piles of strangely aloof "stuff" by Thorne Warhol; Warhol Pure's compelling and really good first book of Berriganesque poetry; the haunting streets of haunting Paris as recreated in West New York, by P.A.P. (Perfect American Products, Inc.).

[A spokeswoman for P.A.P. notes that those who would like to see where "The Haunting Streets" was designed and crafted are welcome to visit the workshop, but she warns that West New York is "actually in New Jersey, which, like, we *love* it."]

PYTHAGORAS

A large sunlit wall dominates the top floor of the new Iconocult Museum, the much-visited and remarked-upon *New York Times Arts & Leisure* wall. We see, just inside the south entrance, and to the left, various manifestations, images, and reproductions of duplications, as well as duplicate reproductions that celebrate, among others, Clint Eastwood, Mikhail Baryshnikov, Philip Glass, Jerome Robbins, and—at long last!—the Kronos Quartet, all against a celebrated background of bakhti, rushdie, bezant, and cold-pressed colluvium. This astounding juxtaposition of material and memoir prepares us for the disparate materials on Igor Stravinsky, Wynton Marsalis, Steve Martin, Leonard Bernstein (and the poetry of *Carousel* and *West Side Story*), along with a heavily annotated and revised typescript of an essay by Woody Allen on the "poetry of David Mamet's dialogue" and the lore of the clarinet. Just beyond these joyously eclectic "heapings," the Public Broadcasting System offers a film of crusty Cornish farmers and their heroic struggles with ovine AIDS, set amid the green hills of Bandore and Deodar. The families, as seen in photographic chronologies, of Steven ("the genius") Spielberg, Arthur Miller, and Woody ("the shy genius") Allen, inhabit a quietly hip corner, wherein a subtle democracy of good taste prevails. A film loop of the greatest scenes from Robert Altman's *The Big Sleep* plays continuously on the ceiling. On a field of semi-conceptualized phosgene waste are "home-movie" stills of Leonard Bernstein, Sting, and Carly Simon, each of them warmly greeting and entertaining Wynton Marsalis and his New Casa Loma Orchestra, and in one playful image, we see, if we look closely, Leonard Bernstein greeting himself! Next, we encounter a jazz collage, detailing the history of jazz from the days of Buddy Bolden, the New Orleans legend, to giants such as John Coltrane, Miles Davis, Thelonious Monk, and Wynton Marsalis, along with a handful of others who have made jazz America's music. A consistently interesting section of wall near the jazz exhibit proffers small cards upon which are printed the effusive comments of celebrities of the arts on their relationship to and love of jazz: among them are Marilyn Monroe, Beverly Sills, the managerial team of the Met, the Modern, and the Whitney, Jim Carrey, Leonard Bernstein, and many others, not least of whom is Norman Mailer. Symphony Sid's ticket stubs for a production of *West Side Story* are mounted next to a glassine portrait of W. A. Mozart, of whom much too little has been written of late. The short film depicting Paul McCartney sitting for a portrait by Andy Warhol, the Warholian atelier one that is rife with artificial beguines, freshens the palate, so to speak, and the viewer is ready to confront the posters, designed by David Hockney, from an idea by Eddie Murphy, for the new PBS

Mystery series, *A Dying in Tartonburyshire,* a brilliant, dark film based on a novel by E. M. Forster, *Howard's Journey.* Anglophilia is also quietly represented by Twyla Tharp's dance to the music of Leonard Bernstein's *Paris Gypsy,* a subtle *hommage* to Gertrude Stein, Virginia Woolf, and Virgil Thomson. There is, most definitely, a shock in store for the assiduous viewer, as he moves from the staid and classically adventurous to the next exhibit, a brilliant montage of outtakes from the sizzling "underground" film made by Andy Warhol, Jack Smith, and Kenneth Anger, *Blond Pussy,* starring Anita Ekberg, Diana Dors, and Jayne Mansfield, each of whom plays Marilyn Monroe mimicking Louise Brooks. Lost for years, *Pussy* must have been a playful romp, one that permits and even encourages art to satirize sex, sex to satirize art, dance to satirize our current moment, and sex to satirize love. In its one screening, it all but silenced the savage gallery of critics at Cannes. Its sole print was purchased by Pablo Picasso, and was last rumored to be in the collection of J. D. Salinger. Speaking of Picasso reminds one, of course, of Henri Matisse, and then, surely, of Roy Lichtenstein: Picasso, Matisse, Lichtenstein—which is greatest, and can we ever know? Miniature reproductions of some of these masters' representative works go a long way toward helping the viewer to a decision. Representative action figures from a myriad of lead-based nauridium renderings show Picasso and Matisse gazing at the only known photograph—a sepia masterpiece!—of the two canny masters at a baseball game at Chicago's Wrigley Field. (Photo on loan from the family of Al Capone.) The artists' Continental mouths are stuffed with a Chicago delicacy, rutabaga sausage, and their eyes are filled with the sadness known only to those who follow the Cubs. Abstract Expressionism is here, too, embodied, so to speak, in an amorphous splash of color, two unevenly matched bilbos, and a 1940 treatise on exology, reputedly an early work by Leonard Bernstein, one that he famously characterized as a "bibelot," and that became, so rumor has it, the basis for his precedent-shattering *Showboat Story*. This remark, in and of itself, may possibly be an inside joke by Al Pacino, a quiet balletomane, here shown in a candid photo as "Mister Hollywood, USA," a refreshing jape, indeed. The New York City Ballet is clustered in a compact haze of sweat, powder, and resin at the far end of the PBS "side" of the wall, catching its collective breath after a thrilling performance of Mozart's "La Bregmata" (K. 12493776529.7) in a new version by Jerome Robbins, George Balanchine, and Sting, with the assistance of Twyla Tharp and in a "black concerto" orchestration by Wynton Marsalis. It is here that visitors like to rest a moment before going on to the exhibits that feature Carol Burnett, Carol Channing, and Ethel Merman, "geniuses of comedy." Arthur Miller, George Lucas, and Robert Altman smile from the midst of a massive three-dimensional collage, "The Holocaust: Years of Hope," that hangs from the Frank Lloyd Wright-inspired ceiling, and that twists, sways, and turns above a series of jagged colporteurs; the sight is, arguably, enough to "make a believer out of just anyone," as Zubin Mehta, David Mamet, and Leonard Bernstein insist. A creased and somewhat faded snapshot of Herbert Von Karajan, in SS dress blacks, leading a small kazoo band of Hitler Youth in a rendition of "We'll Meet Again," for the

Führer, has a disturbing sweetness about it, a "boys' vacation" aura, one that successfully tempers the faux daguerrotype of a thoughtfully scowling Ayn Rand, her Mont Blanc "Aristocrat" pen in one hand and her bailey in the other. A balloon above the famed author-philosopher's head contains the cryptic message, "WHITHER FREEDOM?" The words become ever more mysterious when we learn from an accompanying wall plaque that they were added to the photograph by J. D. Salinger, when he was but thirteen, and "in thrall," as a boyhood friend, on condition of anonymity, put it, "to Greta Garbo's pants." "Erotica" is the title of the last section of the exhibit, and a video loop, *XXXyco,* is erratically projected on the ceiling in a series of spasmodic flickerings based upon the orgasmic patterns of "several film stars." The video, which leaves nothing to the imagination, displays cleverly animated representations of Marilyn Monroe, Virginia Woolf, Igor Stravinsky, and many others, in, as Barbara Kruger's sublimely and hypnotically monotonous voice intones, "THE UNABASHED ACTION OF TRUE ART." In the long corridor that leads to the quiet refreshment garden, a dozen lightly clad young women smear themselves with excrement gathered from homeless shelters, and a sign that runs the entire length of the corridor proclaims, in the best seriocomic Krugeresque fashion, SHIT IS NOT CHOCOLATE. The warm bludgers at the garden exit gate are complimentary, and are made, we are told, from a recipe found among the papers of Leonard Bernstein, who may make an appearance on the exhibition's final day, according to Michael Ovitz and others.

RICCIOLI

Buffalo gals in deerskin doublets edged with lace doubloons, old dog Tray pissing up a rope, sweet Betsy from Pike doing the dirty dongola as only she can do it, waiting to come while her love lies dreaming. "Oh, happy day," proclaims the balloon afloat above the iconic scene. The three kings of the Orient waltzing 'round the mulberry bush, nearer, or so they seem to holler in their barbaric tongue, their God to something. The banners proclaim HOLY! HOLY! HOLY! LORD GOD ALMIGHTY!, and MARYLAND MY MARYLAND, Christ knows why. The vacant chair, direct from Killarney, that wee broth of a skibberreen o'rooney darraghmaight, is here too, upon which rests an authentic McChughrghaighch who looks a good deal like Johnny Schmoker, the idiot savant inventor of the Sweet 'n' Low brassiere ("Make His Eyes Pop the Fuck Out!"). Dixie, while pining away in the midst of a magnolia morass for the dumbo Johnny, is being ogled by old black Joe, who not only saw sweet Nellie home, but threw her one, yet it's never enough, is it?, never, *never* enough for the dark secret blood bubblin' an' boilin', like animals!, half-African and a yard long! Good to know that vacant Johnny will pen a note that begins "Just before the battle, Mother," so the foxed diary here exhibited proveth, testament to the fact that he'd probably forgotten, blessedly, old Joe's hot, bloodshot eyes glued to his snow-white Dixie's delectable diddles, all p-proud and unashamed in their noble nakedness. A beautiful dreamer was young Mr. Schmoker, thus his ass got blowed off by a can of goober peas used in lieu of grapeshot by General La Paloma, the scourge of the upper Potomac, the lower Potawotamie, the Elysian Fields, and the Dakota Breaks. And here, by jinkies, is the "Iron Dove" hisse'f, tenting on the old campground, in a rather shockingly frank sepia study. Who woulda thunk that "the old brown church" was army slang for reckless poguing, much of it having to do with manly yet lissome young recruits from fabled Texas, land of arroyos and coños? Who? (The catalogue, usually explicit, does not hint at what "dry bones" refers to; nor does it suggest a possible reading of the barracks activity referred to as "the ould sod shuffle.") Sweet Genevieve Muldoon, in her best whorehouse finery, is depicted pissing into a little brown jug, as a participant in a famed contest held each year in the midst of the Vienna woods, under the auspices of "whispering hope" Schutz, who is depicted, in a series of linoleum acid-stencil "renderings," costumed as Romeo and Juliet, Reuben and Rachel, Liza Jane Patkowitz, the Fisk Singers, Frankie and Johnny California, Amos and Andy, Joe DiMaggio, and Fiorenza Ziegfeld. These were taken, from the life, as they say, during various stages of Miss Schutz's exhilarating career of bump, tickle, slap, grind, frig, suck, hump, and bugger. For some as yet unexplained reason, the disturbingly graphic images of Miss Schutz "in action" are collectively entitled "Onward, Christian Soldiers." In the second gallery, a bartered bride, clad in nothing but black silk stockings, blue garters, and pink satin pumps is performing a "John Henry" on the entire Mulligan Guard, two or three at a time already! "Silver Threads among the Gold" is *its* wholly opaque title, and tells us nothing of the bride's feelings; although one might surmise that she hankers for the life of the carefree cafonella, the Vienna woods be damned! She is, as some wag once noted, home on the range in these captured moments of sweaty bliss, that is, quoth the sly dog, "heating up a fellow's dinner is her constant delight." And even grandfather's clock rang its ancient chimes at the sight of the flushed bride in her gentle squirm atop the stove. "*I'll* take you home again, Kathleen," for this was Miss S.'s handle, was the astonished cry of the libido-frenzied youths, each wearing the hats their fathers wore, each with a rose of Killarney in his buttonhole, each lost in impure fantasies in the gloaming. "What a friend we have in Jesus," a muscular fellow unaccountably murmured, and was immediately set upon by a chopsticks-wielding Oriental lad, who crooned, during the attack, something that sounded like "aloha oe, aloha oe," later translated by the captain of the H.M.S. *Pinafore* as "where [was] Moses [when the] lights [went] out?" Nearby this fascinating and instructional panorama, we may descry a curious figure, jocularly called Little Buttercup, a lad of progressive secular tastes for his time, and one highly conversant with the contents of *The New York Times Book Review* (known in the review industry as "The Skidmore Fancy Ball"), and *The New Yorker* (smiled upon as "Songs My Mother Taught Me and Taught Me and Taught Me"). Little Buttercup, when he was but a tyke, along with some of the other "babies" on the block, wore golden slippers, and in the evening by the moonlight heard, oh heard dem bells! (Dey be old black Joe's bells.) This was, of course, long before Buttercup hit the old Chisholm Trail and discovered that the notion that there was but one mo' ribber to cross 'fore Loch Lomond, Californiay, hove into view, was no more than a canard, a fib, a runaround, an editor's rejection letter, a "Norwegian steam engine," and a shocking lie. Yet Buttercup pressed on, as numerous photographs show us, dressed now as a Spanish cavalier, now as an estudiantina, now as Stéphanie Gavotte, "La Pajera." "Goodbye, my love, goodbye!" someone supposedly sobbed, while the passionate crowd threw sweet violets, Nellie's blue eyes, voices of spring, a pansy blossom or two, and a handful of earth from Mother's Grave (this last but a figure of speech known as a "clementine"). Climbing up the golden stairs to the third and most breathtaking gallery, the viewer is immediately struck by a tableau showing—to the life—Polly Doodle strolling through the park one day on white wings, so to speak, heading toward a big rock candy mountain because of what the catalogue notes term "the letter that never came." A muscular gladiator follows Miss Doodle like a swan in España, or like Little Annie Rooney, or perhaps like Scheherazade, his eyes flashing the message, "if you love me, darling, tell me with your eyes."

He guessed, surely, in his bursting Eyetalian heart, that love would find a way like a big pizza pie finds its ineffable way down Santo's t'roat, hey! Sadly, the way, for him, was long and over the waves. *Semper fidelis* was the brawny rogue's motto, credo, dado, and blitzen, along with his favorite question to the fair sex, one that clings perpetually to his lips: "Where did you get that hat?" He was a reg'lar down-west McGinty. Next to the winsome and somewhat sad tale of Miss Doodle and her doughty admirer, is a small epic, housed in a glass-topped case, and entitled, rather puzzlingly, "The Thunderer." Here is a photograph of Jimmy "Throw 'im Down" McTater, doing a Polovetsian dance in the garb of his native Bowery, with a denizen of that infamous purlieu, Molly O—short for O'Spud. This is the notorious photo concerning which a pardon came too late to spare the lensman, little "Boy" Blue, from being trampled to death by the march of the raging dwarfs. Another image from that era of loose morals, tight trousers, and see-through skirts shows McTater and Molly as two little girls in blue, both wearing flattering huckleberry "do's." When the roll is called up yonder, so Vesti LaGiubba cracked, they'll be admitted as the waltz of the flowers—"one a peach and the other a pansy." The final presentation, a photocollage, recreates the frenzied world of Dunderbeck, Texas, home of the honeymoon march, sometimes called the humoresque half-step, or, more crudely, the pull-me-off-in-Buffalo. Shown are women whose lovely hair is hanging down their lovely backs, each protected, in a manner of speaking, by the pseudonym, "Margery Daw." One is revealed in shamefully demeaning acts of routine housework, much of it in the kitchen with Dinah (whose Rastus is, yassuh!, usually on parade). The streets of filthy Cairo saw no harsher labor, the sunshine of noisome Paradise Alley illumined faces no sweatier or grimier, not even, for goodness' sake, on Poverty Row. There were, clearly, no creatures more badly used than the poor sluts and pot-wallopers who slaved as "Margery Daw," each and every one. America, beautiful America, is what they yearned to see, or to but hear the bells and ogle the belles of Avenue A; but "King" Cotton March, a vile lecher and taskmaster, urged them to backbreaking labor. "Your sweetheart," he would mock, "your only sweetheart's the man in the moon, you little pussies," he would bellow at each exhausted girl as he mounted her, while she continued her labors. It is quite obvious from these disturbing images that nothing was done to assist these young women, for one can see, if one looks closely at the last photograph of the series, a group of sullen musicians herded together for the monthly Dunderbeck football-and-strawberry social, directed by one Cotton March, Esquire. And the band played on.

[MONTAGES ARRANGED ACCORDING TO BURLOWSKI'S "THEORY OF CHANCE ALIGNMENTS"]

ROOK MOUNTAINS

MODA MILLENNIUMA FOR SPRING: La Verne's new glittering array of silk shirts in vibrant, slambang colors, boldly inspired by the works of famed abstract painter, Mark Rothko, whom La Verne says that she has "just adored" since she first encountered his thrillingly pulsing blob-like shapes; Chic Keaton's profligate dazzle of skirt stylings, sexy and marvelous drapes patterned directly on the "wonderful architecture" of famed abstract painter Piet Mondrian's "Manhattan" pictures; famed abstract painter Jackson Pollock's tragic yet inspiring representations of his teeming tragic emotions and repressed homoeroticism are brought to tingling life in the hipper, "less unfriendly" versions to be discovered in the "urbopolitan" bedding designs of Percy de Abramowicze; the primal, deeply honest, abidingly tough, slashingly calligraphic strokes of famed abstract painter Franz Kline's *hommages* to unknown Japanese masters, as well as to his Polish-German coal-miner parents, discover a new, quietly content life in the warmly masculine and chastely acerbic spring loungewear collection by Renatita Iglioni, the "queen of the pointed tongue" turned fashion giantess; the unlikely and even somewhat disturbing stylistic marriage of famed abstract painters Willem de Kooning and Jasper Johns, astonishingly breathes forth jagged yet strangely beautiful designs for beachwear, cruise togs, and lingerie, whose strong hints of unbridled fetishism will surely renovate the slightly faded glamour of ChiChi Van de Conte, justly notorious for his "Tiny Tits" swimsuits for serious dieters; although famed abstract painter Andy Warhol has been, by rag-trade consensus, "fucking worn out already," his mythical Campbell and Brillo forms, seen through the immaculate eyes of Alameda de Las Pulgas, become brilliant motifs for her line of lushly tinted boxer shorts and T-shirts, which permit us to "like question the nature of art and talent anew," and "ditto," says Ms. de Las Pulgas, for famed abstract painter Pablo Picasso, and his masturbatory obsessions; and, finally, there is what can only be called the stone-bitchin' hottest of the spring shoe stylings, the Guston Klunkers, as Sueda Vochsse, marketing director for Bruttafigura of Milano, has slyly dubbed them. "We're virtually certain that these shoes, boldly based on forms first developed by famed abstract painter Philip Guston, will be the most sought-after fashion statement of the season. It's quite humbling to realize that craftsmen bootmakers, like those at Bruttafigura, can make great, inspired art even greater and more inspired by means of vision and world-class craft and persistence and Old World devotion to excellence, all linked to a first-class marketing campaign and a few blow jobs in the right place and at the right time—only kidding!" The Klunkers will be suitable for walking, sitting around, and power napping, Ms. Vochsse notes.

SEA OF CLOUDS

Black-light lamps, placed carefully around the room, and selected, as you surely know, with the sneer that passes for witty irony in this sophisticated time of the businessman-comedian-writer-host-actor, illuminate found objects—salutes to the gauche past—that clutter the place: Regrets and mercies, taxes and napalm, sex and marriage, installment plans and out-of-tune pianos and cauliflower, the end of the road, the end of the game, the end of the party, and four o'clock in the rainy morning; gravestones in Brooklyn, bitter-cold funerals, wet black trees, rubber soles in hospital corridors, oxygen tents; the sun on the beach and on that beach and on the other beach; the smell of clean hair, awed love, thighs and bathing suits, dumb lust; whatnots, snots and sneezes and coughs and dark-brown blood; c-rations, lustrous carbines smelling of gun oil, combat boots and smudged brass and the snap and whine of .50 caliber slugs overhead, canned fruit salad on the mashed potatoes; old photos, yellowed lace, a black mantilla, spatulas, cooking spoons, wood-handled forks, cast-iron skillets with black silken innards; cannoli, cassata, oil and garlic on the fusilli and a bright drift of parsley; gas refrigerators, wooden potato mashers, long dark hallways and musty hampers, leg of lamb, string beans, boiled potatoes, green mint green jelly green, a two-way stretch girdle and Evening in Paris; the sun on Sheepshead Bay; lanolin wild root brylcreem vitalis vaseline and torn underwear, smiling mouths, straw boaters, creamy vests, Packards, DeSotos, Hudsons, LaSalles, and flat packs of English Ovals; whiteness of Twenty Grands, Sweet Caporals, Wings, Herbert Tareytons, Virginia Rounds, not to mention heartbreak loneliness and despair; lies and self-pity, questions and sobs and wails and regrets and death; flowers, recriminations; priests in black and gold and crepuscular churches, candles and incense and the gleaming monstrance, censers and Jesus Christ Almighty and Sister Veronica; sweet perfume and sweat, sweet odor of thighs and breasts, of young women in flat straw hats and spring coats, of virginity; the wind come up off the Narrows, fish and salt, clean, remote, sound of buoys distant, and the bridge, a drawing in the haze and fog, and the barely recalled laughter of dead women. "Don't see nothin' too goddamn funny *here*."

SEA OF COLD

Death loves a mystery. Death can't get started. Death in high heels. Death makes the world go 'round. Death in a Class A uniform. Death at the Dakota. Death your magic spell is everywhere. Death is here to stay. Death goes to the movies. Death is marching on. Death travels to Samarra. Death and his pal, Destruction. Death loves to kiss you good night. Death makes the heart grow fonder. Death dislikes magazines. Death only has eyes for you. Death is back in town. Whatever Death wants, Death gets. Death is where you find it. Death in the rain, Death in a blue dress, Death in Havana. Death on the golden sands. Death says "hi" to Bunky. Death and taxes, Death and taters, Death in Texas. Death to intelligence. Death to bad art. Death is a little bit of heaven. Death in Venice. Death in Des Moines. Death makes a deal. Death is a bitch. Death is a bastard. Death makes a lot of sense. Death fears no man. Death is a consumer, a sap, and a sucker. Death goes along singing a song. Death on a pale horse. Death hates all religions. Death don't like ugly. Death can't run in the mud. Death laughs at life. Death bes not proud. Death likes to hone his craft. Death walked right in. Death gets that old feeling. Death don't want no peas and rice and coconut oil. Death he's got no bananas. Death eats antipasto twice. Death needs killin'. Death and modern English usage make a great team. Death sends a little gift of roses. Death couldn't have done it without the guys. Death and the end of the novel in love. Death and history, Death and love, and fun at the county fair. Death goes to the country. Death don't get around much anymore. Death takes a course in creative writing. Death walks the dog and rocks the cradle. Death in grey flannel. Death marching marching on the burning sands. Death in Central Park. Death in love with love. Death gazes long into the mirror. Death bids farewell to the old gang. Death enters the sweepstakes, plays the lottery, bets a saw on a long shot, draws to an inside straight, and craps out over and over again. Death is pissed off. Death loses all the time. Death boils bagels. Death fries eggs. Death discovers girls. Death discovers boys. Death will hump anything. Death is gay sort of. Death at the end of the tunnel. Death saw you last night. Death scrambles eggs. Death in Glocca Morra. Death invents a couple of new diseases. Death loves to tango. Death returns to the South. Death in the French Quarter, in Brownsville, in Dyker Heights, in Ozone Park, in Tottenville, in the pool and ocean, river and creek. Death takes away the sweet. Death plays a kazoo. Death chewin' on a cracker. Death don't give a fuck about you or me or anybody else, or all arrogance of earthen riches.

Art from the Transcontinental Traveling AIDS Project

SEA OF CRISES

A Film

Black night, black rain falling outside the windows of a brightly lighted room, within which a meeting has come to a barely discernible order. "A meeting about what?" A man, obviously a real-estate agent by the look of his too-expensive tie and shoes, not to mention the Mont Blanc pen in his shirt pocket, rises to address the people in attendance, who shout at him despite a pinched-face, cadaverous woman's call for order and decorum for God's sake. What is her name? And what gruesome diet has she embraced to make her resemble a handful of broken straws, to make her legs so pitifully thin that her stockings bag and wrinkle at knees and ankles? The Auschwitz diet? And what is the real-estate agent's name? "I don't understand this part of the picture, especially the fat man who has appeared in the doorway on the right." The starved woman looks at the fat man, not understanding his presence in the doorway. Has not this door always been closed? "Are these horrible people supposed to be *tenants?*" The real-estate agent has removed his tie and shoes, and plans, or so it would seem, to speak. The tenants rise and begin to dance. "Did they dance like *that* back in the old days?" What old days? There is a sign on the wall (seen for the first time) that notes, in large black letters, NO VACAN-CIES. Where is it stated, in what contract or its bylaws, that such signs are even permitted in impromptu meetings such as this one? "Stated?" Black night now enters the room at last, preceded by black rain and the usual bitter cold. "Ain't California, man." The tenants have left. The real-estate agent gives his skeletal assistant a kiss as she reads from a book of mediocre feminist poems, *Purple Gentian*. "Who is the author of this lousy book?" Fake soldiers in Class B khakis enter the room, their brass dull and smudged, their patches and chevrons sewn on crookedly, their shoes scuffed and spotted with what looks to be dried vomit and Christ only knows what else. "These guys are *soldiers?*" They stand out starkly against the black night, starkly and a little artily. The room is, let us be clear about it, a freight elevator, in which the skinny woman, her lips swollen with sexual excitement, gazes at her boss, who is now a different man altogether, one who pretends that his name is not Arthur, the name that his amorous assistant calls him by. "Is this guy the same guy as the guy before with the tie?" Thus the indispensable magic of cutting-edge cinema, so they buzz, buzz and trumpet. "Buzz and—wotthefuck?—trumpet?" The elevator stops at the sub-sub-basement and the doors open onto an *echoing and dimly lighted parking garage.* NO VACANCIES trumpets the sign on the wall, a sign that may well have been transported from an earlier place, or scene. And yet, the garage, echoing and dim, is virtually empty of automobiles, another mysterious image, or at least symbol. "For like, life?" The tenants, however, have all gathered here, and they are once again shouting at Arthur in a language that is not comprehensible, even though it is clear that Arthur and his flushed assistant, who has quite shamelessly removed most of her clothing, not only understand it, but are repelled by it. The fat man, it is now apparent, is the tenants' leader, although he pretends to be raptly studying a diagram of the sub-sub-basement, whose only legible words, at this distance, read: *You Are Here*. "Is that the name of the movie?" The real-estate agent is speaking quietly to his gal Friday, whom the fat man is ogling. "Maybe she's the real-estate guy's wife." Wife or no, Arthur seems to think that she is some dish, as does the fat man, bony though she may be. "It's always the way." the parking garage is now filled with cars, and the NO VACANCIES sign at last makes sense, even though there may well be *some* vacancies. At least the shiny machines look like cars, but you never know, you never know. In any event, they are not, as Arthur's eager enamorata attests, *art!* Despite the stares of the tenants and the fat man, she is, as the phrase has it, all over Arthur, and dizzy with lust. How she'd rather be in her favorite Village "pub," sitting across from Arthur, their eyes locked above their tomato martinis, speaking of art and life and love, and, well, serious things in general. Love, sizzling love, would follow, in due course. "Is this, I mean this whole thing like, art?" Black night absorbs the entire shebang.

SEA OF FERTILITY

The garden exhibition that opened at the T. C. Andrews galleries on Saturday arrives here from Los Angeles and Houston, and it is well worth waiting for. Occupying the South Patio and Mower Gardens of the ground-floor gallery, it is a delight to the eye. Glossy-black Orient dew, surrounded by a pale-golden halo of rare, Sacred dew, suggests the moon's bosom, bared, all unashamedly, to avid blowing roses of variegated colors and lush, foreign-bred, purple flowers. Sweet leaves and green blossoms inform a grassy slope, brilliant under lights especially designed for this exhibition by Garden Glows of London and Manchester. It is as if the gallery has been given over to an eternal spring, one which enamels all its contiguous elements, one which, in effect, "enamels everything," as someone, with a gesture toward elegant panache, once remarked. There are also in attendance, so to speak, bright oranges in at least a dozen varieties, gleaming like so many golden lamps in the subtle yet spectacular lighting, a magical illumination that, in this breathtaking corner of the garden, creates what seems an uncanny green night. Figs, real or made of the most exquisitely fragile Baccarat crystal, seem to be at our mouths everywhere, as we move through the gorgeous displays; and melons—golden, orange, mauve, cerise, azure, brilliant yellow—crowd together at our feet in profligate and splendid profusion. Apples, cedars, the huge pomegranates called "Chinese honeymoons," each bursting with jewels, awaken a kind of vegetable love in the viewer, and cool fountains contrast their silvery sprays with deep green shadows. There is Venus, in her pearly boat, redolent of strange perfumes, beautiful and regal as the Marvel of Peru, the legendary tulip (one of which was valued at the cost of a thousand prize sheep and a famed actor); and dazzling daffodils, arranged in careless garlands of repose, charm and soothe the eye. And at the far wall is a lavish collage—the curious peach, by the hundreds, amid its delicate and delicious aroma, strewn amid the shadows of countless roses and indigo violets. Every element—form, color, arrangement, scent—of this marvelous exhibition takes its place in an equally marvelous prospect of fruits, of grasses, and of flowers.

SEA OF MOISTURE

1. We see Private First Class Earl Fruchter in the shower room of a Mexican whorehouse, the realms of gold, if you please, with Nora, Elvira, Isabel, and Margot. All are naked, all are wet, all are glowing in the steam, all are laughing.

2. Just down the hall in this establishment, Ofelia's, in the large "salon," that contains the bar and dance floor, Private First Class Sklar rests his elbows on a table, while the sixteen-year-old Purita, her skin a creamy tan, bends her sizzling glance, in wild surmise, upon him—and what enamored bride in the drowsy numbness of a honeymoon morning, ever looked so lovingly upon her exhausted groom?

3. Yet Sklar, along with Sergeant First Class Eddie Trainor, a medical-aid man late of the badly mauled 24th Infantry Division, faces all aflame, are being sexually fondled by the forever panting Lola, of El Paso and Piedras Negras, she of the pastel chiffon cocktail dresses, matching heels, and faint acne scars. Sklar and Trainor groan as Señorita Lola leaves off her expert manual attentions, since she, as Corporal Whitehouse once put it, "ceases upon the midnight."

4. Color photographs, in a snappy collage, reveal a passel of exuberantly drunken soldiers, in khakis and the flowered garments known as "AWOL shirts," madly dancing with their chosen whores, and the noise made by these revelers can easily be imagined; at a table in the crepuscular rear of the room depicted, and barely discernible

5. in these images that pretend to offer us the truth about the febrile disturbance of young libidos, is Paulina, who may be remembered by some as the Indian girl partial to ice blue underwear, which sets off her silken-gold thighs to perfection, and which makes her a local bright star, christened, by Sergeant Beldino, Señorita Lingerie.

6. What wild ecstasy for Private Archie Griffith to pretend that Paula is his fiancée, his as-yet-unravished bride, his Judy or Barb, this tall, dark girl,

7. who will not remove her brassiere and thus grant Private Griffith the sight of his fair Joan's ripening breast; and so, in leaden-eyed misery, he pays Paula an extra dollar if she will leave her stockings on, so as to assure himself of her profession; for what fair wife in Private Griffith's native town of Belleville, Illinois, would go to amorous bed so flagrantly deshabille?

8. Rills of crimson wine and spiced cold mushrooms have no place amid the raucous, sweaty, fevered lusts and drunken laughter of Ofelia's; nor of the 1-2-3 Club, the Palma de Oro, Señora Amor's, and the Cadillac, but are substituted for by icy Carta Blanca cerveza and bowls of salty green olives.

9. This dark photograph—there is no light to speak of— shows Celia, Visitación, Teresa, and Clarita smiling in the

darkness, their teeth gleaming whitely, their naked bodies in sweet repose, the dull opiate of a night's sweated wages protecting them from starvation, illness, brutality, the clap, and even poisoned wine, for yet another day.

10. Some soldier, passed out on the floor of the Club Mosaic, the last oozings of his last bout of mescal nausea pooled by his all-American chin, dreams of

11. flies on summer eves, of downy owls, and of the face of the carelessly beautiful whore, Julia Emilia Suarez. He sighs. He will marry the fucking lovely bitch, for he loves her, and she be fair; more happy love (and she be fair!).

12. We come to understand these things, for Jenny Shuttleworth-Robson, an assistant professor of cultural studies at Johns Hopkins, has explained the gestures and signs and obscured metonymies of the photographs and cinematic "stills" in this "BORDERTOWN" exhibition, in her introductory essay to its sumptuous catalogue. Professor Shuttleworth-Robson is a recognized expert in the everyday lives of what she has termed "brothel-entertainment workers," but what the whores themselves call *schifuzza,* or, more informally, *schifuzz'* or *schi'*. Nobody has determined how the Italian word has come to be used the world over.

BORDERTOWN: Loves and Lives in Mexico: *To December 31st.*

SEA OF NECTAR

The Transgressive Act

Fourteen motherfucking beer bottles are fucking haphazardly arranged next to an off-white shitty wall on the left. Six fucking more are fucking lined up in front of the fucking off-white wall on the right, in the foreground, you got it, cuntface? Four more are over here, right fucking *here,* next to this, you cocksucker! There are also twenty-six bottles in the back, and, just behind those fuckers, thirteen more. Nearby, shithead, two bottles lie on their sides, and one fucking hangs from the fucking ceiling, just above them, or above that, shiteater. Twenty-one are behind the false wall that has been hinted at in the hip ads placed in those faggot shitrags, and God knows how many more are fucking hidden under those things to the left, prick. A few more fucking bottles are fucking crowded together and the cocksucking motherfucker prick bastard clutter right in fucking front of that cunt of a woman standing there grinning like a possum eating shit also seems to be a fucking part of it all, the asshole shit! Forty more of the motherfuckers are here and there, and even more, if one should take a fucking look! The fucking glare of the fairy-ass lights make all these useless shit-heel things fucking shine and fucking gleam and fucking glint and fucking God knows fucking what, like nobody's business, understand, you bull-dyke cuntlapping bitch? "Nobody's Business" is the putative title of this pile of putrid shit "installation," designed to make the assholes of the fucking world think they're in art fucking heaven, although "Shit for Brains" would fit the fucking mess better; the title, incidentally, you dumb fuck, following, in what prickheads call "a new tradition," the nickname bestowed on the cutting-edge artist who "made" this stinking whorehouse of a layout, the cocksucker faggot fairy queer prick motherfucker! That's what they call him, "Shit for Brains," don't kill the messenger, cunthead, everybody knows it. It is, let's face it, a fucking bad, really bad piece of fucking bullshit art, right, ass-fucker? Fucking A!

SEA OF RAINS

A curiosity that attracts what many exhibition-arts experts have called its "fair share" of visitors, whom it invariably leaves amused, irritated, or bewildered, is the so-called "editorial wall," a display that contains fragments of editorial correspondence, sent by various editors, over a period of some thirty-five years, to the agent of a writer who is called, so as to protect his privacy, "B." It is beyond the scope of this article to present the messages on the editorial wall in their entirety, but a representative sampling from them should serve to give their overall flavor, or, as one writer recently put it, their "odor." Without further introductory remarks, then:

I've always admired B's work, as you know, but this handcart doesn't look as if it's going to make us any lettuce, not, as you know, that General Motors Xerox Publishing Group Ltd, puts lettuce above good, fresh art.

I doubt if I could make this wholly unreadable slag— save, of course, for its marvelous descriptions of things— a success.

B, as you know, can only, alas, be marketed as a good soldier, not, alas, as the perfect stunner of a planet that readers, alas, demand today.

B's new novel is compellingly urgent, but it is not intriguingly powerful or astonishingly compelling. Sorry.

I know how highly regarded B is among literary circles, but I'm afraid that his somewhat difficult work is just not right for Shit House at the present time.

I read B's sickeningly erotic book with as much lust as I could muster, but I doubt that I am the right whore to do right by it. Best of luck to B.

The pages, one by one, are fine pages, as are the words, one by one, but I feel that the pages and the words together don't make me want to put my shoulder to the wheel for B's fine new novel.

Fine plumbing, as is all of B's work, yet unrelentingly odious and morbidly attentive to gross details of things.

I admit that I pissed my designer pants reading this one, but after the laughter, there was nothing much to "dig" into.

This schlub of a book, bright in spots, of course, doesn't fit our grandiose fictional plans as of now.

As you well know, I lack the brains and finely honed reading skills required to publish B's book with the care it deserves, since I am currently sort of really fucked up with a monster coke habit.

It gives me, as you may know, a big hard-on to regularly read your better authors, like B, and as regularly reject them.

B's new entry is difficult, boring, and sexually disgusting and misogynistic, but it, as you know, has passages of lyric fireworks. Not for us, I'm afraid, as you know.

B's—let's face it—"literary" book doesn't fit well into the context of our poor list as it now stands, nor, for that matter, as it will stand at any time in the foreseeable future.

How I'd love to be able to grab up B's new blockbuster, but my hands are tied, as are my knees and ankles, alas!

If B had another book that we could bring out a year or so before or after this book I'd love to take this book on along with the other book. But as it stands, sorry.

We schmoozed, all of us here at Annex-Subsidiary, about the real strengths of B's new book, but finally the "gals from Swarthmore" here thought it demeaning to educated white women with money.

The latter sixteenth of B's new offering is almost shattering in its power, but the earlier sixteenth seems derivative, weak, unimaginative, hackneyed, and plodding. Give my best to B.

The utter holocaust of B's new exploration of a novel is a marvel of authorial honesty and creative tale-spinning; but, alas, we all felt that it depended much too heavily on stylistic crap rather than straightforward plotting.

In order to do right by B's ludicrous yet oddly disturbing new sally into the perverse, I'd have to feel, on every page, the excitement of being humped on my desk by the spick mail boy, and I just don't.

I'm delighted, as you may know, that you thought to send me B's rubbishy new novel, along with his collection of rotten stories that I so loathed a year ago, but they don't add up to the sort of swill that I envisaged making up a really knockout marketing event. Too bad.

B's new book, we all agreed here, has three pages, two paragraphs, one clause, seven and a half phrases, thirty-seven sentences, and four hundred and sixty-five words of keen, knee-weakening majesty, but the rest of the book is kind of blah, so we figured, "oh, fuck it," alas.

What a remarkable slab of a book this is!—but we have room on our list for only one such slab a year, and this year's loser has already been contracted for. Best to B.

I must confess that I found the plot of B's new offering confusing and elusive, but that's a failing I guess I'll have to live with in this vale of tears.

I liked lots of B's at times extraordinary new novel, but the author seems somewhat too pleased with himself, but perhaps I'm not the right editor for such a difficult work.

B's latest foray into his standard porno-fiction is often elegant and even beautiful, but it lacks the punch of the short-story collection of his that we passed on last year. Thanks so much for letting me see the work of this important author.

B's work simply lacks the dishonesty and superficiality of the work that we cotton to here at Himmler-Aspen, at least in this woman's opinion, and so I'm afraid that I'll have to pass again on this new novel.

We loved, really loved, this excursion into rage and bitterness, but I'm sure that another editor somewhere will love it even more.

It's hard for me to believe that I've held on to B's manuscript for seventeen months, so I'm sending it back to you, still unread, as you know.

I'll have to say no again, I'm sorry to say, to B's terrific new book, since, as you know, Van Cleef & Arpels no longer publishes anything that resembles *books.*

We were impressed by B's sly and ingenious new novel, but we have at least nine really bad books under contract, and are seriously overextended at the present time.

I'm afraid that I have no record of ever receiving B's manuscript of humorous essays. It's been a madhouse here since our merger with Metro Yahoo Collins Spielberg. If I come across it I'll have it returned by messenger immediately.

SEA OF SERENITY

In the haze, there can be discerned, perhaps, a dark grave, an Italian sea, an ideal copy of the lyre of Orpheus, and an arbor of formidable vines among whose bilious green rests a solitary rose of sorrow. Alas! the head they all adore aches still with the kiss of the enormous queen, and what a lariat-spinner she can sardonically be. And there she stands, or, actually, emerges, emerges steadily and slowly from a crepuscular violet and lavender that informs the entire room! There glows, as well, the golden hair that is popular with every true son of Greece, an odd collection of rogues, of course, many of them actually Italian, covered, most usually, with ashes like unto grime on a smeared window, through which most travelers cannot see the horizon. Just as well, since it was never intended that they see anything at all. What a blague! What a jape! A pale-pink hydrangea complements the daguerrotypes of the azure sea, although "azure" is a word that creative-writing cliques insist should never be used in, well, *creative writing*. And we are well aware of what that is! As something more than mere decoration, assemblage doyens and their faithful docents claim that a flame-colored scarf is central to just about everything; as are, too, the Lord of the Volcano, three green glass eyes, peace be upon them, two Frostian spondees, dragons' teeth (as usual), and a certain implacable scarlet. None of these earthy, sublunary things can manage (despite their changing dispositions within the space of this really beautiful, if somewhat fruity, fake Louis XVI apartment, complete with upholstered jakes) to derange the pure given whole, the serene quiver of Sacred Art, which is always as astonishing and inevitable, but not really, not really at all, as a song by the sublime Harry Warren, e.g., "At Last" or "I Only Have Eyes for You."

SEA OF TRANQUILLITY

Three clarinets, attached bell to mouthpiece, bell to mouthpiece, bell to mouthpiece, make what might be thought of as a fairly long "tube," glistening black, decorated with what the catalogue is pleased to call, incorrectly, "silver filigree." The tube leans against an off-white wall. Title: "These Silvery Things Are Valves Like." Nothing else appears to be in the gallery, save for an attentive guard, in an (but of course!) "ill-fitting" uniform that could "use the services" (but of course!) of a dry cleaner. We say: "He's his usual *gracious* self!" We say: "He didn't even bother to come to his own farewell party!" We say: "How we gonna give 'im his gift?" The guard examines the clarinets/tube and it becomes clear that he is, or may be, an integral part of the exhibit, like he's *art*. We say: "He's probly *part* of the exhibit, like, art!" We say: "As far as I'm concerned, he can go piss up a rope! Look at that ill-fitting uniform on him, Jesus." The catalogue suggests that the artist who created this majestic piece rarely interacts with his colleagues, but is aloof, disturbingly private, and, in matters aesthetic, his usual *gracious* self. He is a practicing poet, and also the reluctant spokesman for those who love life, laugh over a bottle of good Cabernet, feel that nature is extremely important to all human intercourse as long as it stays out of the driveway, and *attend their own farewell parties.* Alternative titles for the piece, culled from the visitors' book that rests on a lectern at the gallery entrance, are: "Breaking Up of Our Summer Concert," "Orchestra en Plein Vent," "A New Year Contraband Ball at Vicksburg," "Dos a Dos or Rumpti Iddity Ido," and "Sporting a Toe." "And they ask why," a woman, rumored to be the department chairman—and who looks like a bag of rags tied in the middle—says, "*he* makes the big monkey!" A quick check of the monthly-meeting minutes notes that she may have actually said, "the big money," although there are some who argue for the fey, "the bug money." The clamor increases as the academics and their guests await the free box lunches and the mineral water, but the clarinet installation restores silence. For once.

STRAIGHT WALL

A long flat slab of the finest marble from the celebrated
although by now wholly exhausted quarries of the small
Tuscany village of Sfogliatelle is balanced, on one edge, ele-
gantly if precariously, atop a volume of dead poems of some
local notoriety. Their floating vocables urge new ways of seeing if not reading, of reading if not seeing, or of thinking a
little if neither reading nor seeing. So the placard above the
receptionist's desk states: said placard and desk depend from
the saccade-like nervousness and twitchiness of the slab's
darker side. Bolted to the slab are magazines that feature
some of the finest writers of our time, but not, thank God,
all of them. Many of them are in collaboration on contemporary thoughts: "The Future of the Village"; "Frozen
Custard Rediscovered"; "How a Tough Street Kid Became an
Oscar Contender"; and many others. Their prose, which is
refreshingly irreverent, is the norm. The magazines have
been sprayed with a faux-gold lacquer which has then been
"sown," while still wet, with cigarette stubs, ashtrays,
insects, a small Burundi vase, a report detailing the bad news

for an unknown yet beloved person as to his incurable disease, or, perhaps, diseases (the report is in the demotic Greek spoken by Weehawken diner owners), many excellent words from here there and everywhere, a sepia-tone photograph of a small glade in Van Cortlandt Park in the Bronx, smeared with what may be brown paint, Fox's U-Bet chocolate syrup, or excrement, and a glob of a truly ghastly *crème de cervelle,* once served to a Princeton alumnus on the occasion of his life. A small rectangle of stiff white cardboard is stapled to the wall and reads: DON'T BELIEVE THE POOR. The slab lists slightly to one side and is bathed in the soft light that is, so we have been told many and many a time, the hallmark of New England summers. A cheerful video loop reveals a smiling youth gesturing toward what he says, or, rather, shouts, is San Francisco. "WHAT WEATHER!" is a phrase that he repeats over and over again. The slab turns occasionally, somewhat like a *scena ductilis.* But only at certain hours, and not so anyone would notice. Then there is the music that happenstance, as it will, directs, jingle jingle jingle. And all is rendered in a brilliant Lydian translation.

THEOPHILUS

Just opened: At the Kangol-Polo Galleries: You won't go far wrong with this judiciously selected, and soberly, but not stuffily authoritative exhibition of what has recently come to be called "ingenuous" art, or, occasionally, "crippled" art. The show goes a long way toward sorting out the lines and planes, not to mention the arcs and tangents, large circles and even complex rhomboids of influences, affiliations, and imitative procedures to be discerned within this difficult, often misunderstood, and, at times, hopelessly muddled school. Everything is placed simply, even puritanically, in the galleries' spacious rooms, and the whole takes up, quite comfortably, the entire second floor of what was once a SoHo firetrap. The works are arranged in shrewd juxtapositions and canny alliances, so as to allow the viewer to discover how these iconoclastic fringe artists and artisans and their art and artisan products play off each other. The great Rube Chang, for instance, and Marco "the magnificent" Globus present three semi-collaborative works ("Blue Asters and Paperback," "Edward Van de Fugger, Christian," and

"Lieutenant Chip Mainwaring Abusing Himself"), which remind one of the early red-clay-and-torn-denim "cut-downs" made by George, "the soupreem master of magikk," in his Lake Jango garage, as well as the "moron collages" that were discovered a decade ago in a corncrib on Jubal Chamborizee's property. (Chamborizee, also known as Lord Chimborazo or Sir Henry Cotopaxi, was the acknowledged master of sooty-cob annealing, a painstaking process whose subtlest techniques died with him.) Ruth Billbew's "The Beast from the Stygian Deeps," "Larry's Bony Wife, Martha," and "Ants at a Picnic: Study in Black and Egg Yolk," are clearly in the same early-ingenuous mode as Duwayne Bushelle, Bushelle Edwards, Mac Brontus and his humming raccoons (Brontus's droll designation for those who selflessly assist him in his crush-and-burn operations); and her "Vomit in the Doorway," perhaps the central iconic image of all postwar ingenuous art, and an acknowledged focus for contemporary studies of painterly surfaces, especially in the work of Katz, Thiebaud, and, not surprisingly, Warhol, reminds the most jaded gallery-goer of how sublime the "cripples" can be. The powerful construct, "Leventy-Seven," by Duke Charlotte La Bushe, startles anew in its position of majestic prominence in a small gallery off the main corridor, as it gestures toward, illumines, and shrewdly "explains" its immediate successors in the fiendishly difficult heavenly-glaze procedure, "Uniform and Chips, with Pastor," by Whitfield Wamp, "Weightlifters at Prayer," Fincher Leroy Ellerbing's last known work, and "Jesus Destroying Pornography," by an anonymous member of the Southern Baptist Corsairs. The catalogue, informative and entertaining, by the exhibition's curator, Stanford MacArthur, informs and entertains, indeed, yet helps us to remember that which it is dangerous, much like history and current events, to forget; that art is, at its most sublime, simple, decent, and, as one delighted visitor to Kangol-Polo was overheard to say, "easy on the eyes."

TSIOLKOVSKY

"Three (or so) segments of a work in complex progress . . ."

". . . but the myth of the frontier has consistently engaged the disarmingly irreverent sophistication of the modern multi-lens camera, of course. Earlier works, like the focus of the interplay as seen in the presentation of the scrims usually associated with the pinhole camera, the nonchalant stance, the thematic array, and the variously colored fluorescents, confront the secondary myth of the iconic cross-cultural artist, as prefigured in the many seminal and provocative essays by a group of distinguished contributing editors, published in the *Contemporary Camera Obscura*. 'The nearest star,' to adduce a well-known remark of the anonymous Gnostic followers of Blake, 'is much too near,' profoundly encapsulates the varied philosophies of shared visual interests and loosely Hegelian theoretical vistas, many of them here on display as a group for the first time, allowing students and scholars to spend hours, rather than the usual hurried moments, with objects commonly associated with the tenaciously unyielding subjects herein deployed in 'ur'-construc-tions that take as their unifying and irreversible (although sub-ject, always, to aporia) theme the images that are, paradoxically, vital yet moribund. Whereas mechanical tools, e.g., the hammer, the adze, the wood plane, the nathan, the ripsaw, and the blotter, project and valorize the images in the early films of Wynton Marsalis, inescapable filtering of new and little-known earlier works by now-lost 'outsider' cinematographers, as presented in varied locations within North American public spaces throughout the fifties and sixties, contradict a haze of pioneering techniques which can transform such mundane instruments into dazzling media installations that relentlessly transgress the cherished Germanic motifs which inoculate, or, conversely, are inoculated by, surprising Baudelairean *correspondances*; for example, via the imagery of Callahan, Atget, and Adams, cultural *topoi,* so to speak, that have delighted and outraged the 'mouse in the dynamo,' as Bartley Scott put it some years ago, as well, too, as influencing those cinéastes and plasticists who pioneered the fevered pyrotechnics and mysterious and ineradicable film captions that have come to be viewed, with much justification, as harbingers of pure process, emblematic clips heavy with metaphor, and short but multi-layered arguments, not to mention a vertiginous, motile linear perspective and the labile interfaces contemporaneously labeled as 'techno-video interventions,' despite their static modes within . . ."

—*Kelli Dawn Tsiolkovsky*

Kelli Dawn Tsiolkovsky writes the "Arts, Dining, and Cinema" column for the *West Village Edge,* and is also the author of *Brooklyn! Economy for Epicures,* and the forthcoming novel, *Andy Warhol Was a Virgin* (Whitlow/St. Martin's).

TYCHO

A photograph in the corner of the apartment, cloudy, dark, difficult to make out: In a room filled with haze, a woman in a low chair, her face in her hand in a familiar female posture, weeping—again, familiarly—bitterly. She weeps for Buddy, her dead son, killed at the age of sixteen in a fall from the parallel bars that at one time graced, God knows why (perhaps to kill Buddy) every public high-school gym in New York. "My Buddy," she whispers, bitterly weeping. Life, despite its vaunted pleasures, can be monstrous and ruthless, utterly without pity or solace, despite sunsets and cool forests. The days are long since he died, long. The room's haze seems to thin or lighten, but then it is again precisely as it was, so it probably never changed at all. (As if a photograph could show such changes!) She thinks about her son all through the day, the days, every day, her obsession is said to be "unhealthy," an "unhealthy obsession." So much for assistance from friends and providers of assistance. The world, and we know exactly what "the world" is, prefers that everybody rid oneself of anything that might even hint at "unhealthy obsession," no matter the form it may take. It wants everybody to fall in! dress right dress! ready front! cover! You girls gon' soldier or you'll be doin' close-order *all* night! No room for obsessions here, of any sort, that's what "the world" wants. But she misses his voice, she misses the touch of his hand. Maybe she'll come out of this funk, this depression, this despair, and become, once again, a valuable, contributing member of society, with a great deal, oh, a *great deal* to give to same. In the meantime, while society waits, Buddy, her sweet, handsome, funny Buddy, nobody quite so true, is dead; and, although, as a good Catholic, she knows that he must be in heaven with God and all His angels, he's not here. He's not *here!* She thinks about him all through the day. But now, wait, we discover that this is a photograph of—what?—a man shielding his eyes from the sunlight that enters the small room through a worn, almost transparent, window shade. He is thinking about something, but what? He is thinking about the woman whose photograph he is gazing at, holding it at an angle, away from the glare of the sun. She is in a low chair, bitterly weeping. He has looked at the photograph every day for months, an "unhealthy obsession."

WALTHER

Touchdown!: Mayhem for a New Millennium

Fifty years of gridiron history, the glamour, anguish, pain, and courage of this "equivalent to war," as Buster Walter, dean of football writers, put it, the exhibition brought to us with the generous assistance of the Texas Petroleum Products Alliance.

The compelling photographs of the exhibition include classic images, both historical and contemporary, of the adipose guardbacker, blustering backender, cute tackleback, demanding quarterend, egregious endtackle, flouncing puntdrifter, grotesque quarterguard, hallucinatory crawlingback, incendiary nosebacker, jejeune endnoser, knuckleheaded walkback, lascivious endpunter, moronic tackleguard, newfangled halfnose, otiose comingback, precious goingback, queenly tackleblitzer, resistant outback, sincere balltoucher, triumphant pushnoser, underpaid shortflagger, visionary quartercatcher, wonderful widecenter, xenophobic backshover, yawning openguard, and zenlike jingotackle.

Sincere thanks for gracious permission to reproduce their likenesses to Jambo Pierce, Biff Caldwell, Z. Z. Steeples, Derkone Motherwell, Carl Bracciole, El-Hashishe Thompson, Merlon Brown, Lucky Reno, El 'Rode Washington, Ziggy Imbriale, and Calderotte Saunders.

[Proceeds from admissions and sales of souvenirs and memorabilia to go to the Citizens' Committee to Build TEXPROL Stadium: "The People's Place, The People's Pride."]

Lunar Follies was designed at Coffee House Press
in the Warehouse District of downtown Minneapolis.
The text is set in Perpetua with Bittersweet titles.

OTHER BOOKS BY GILBERT SORRENTINO

POETRY
The Darkness Surrounds Us
Black and White
The Perfect Fiction
Corrosive Sublimate
A Dozen Oranges
Sulpiciae Elegidia: Elegiacs of Sulpicia
White Sail
The Orangery
Selected Poems 1958-1980

FICTION
The Sky Changes
Steelwork
Imaginative Qualities of Actual Things
Flawless Play Restored: The Masque of Fungo
Splendide-Hôtel
Mulligan Stew
Aberration of Starlight
Crystal Vision
Blue Pastoral
Odd Number
A Beehive Arranged on Humane Principles
Rose Theatre
Misterioso
Under the Shadow
Red the Fiend
Pack of Lies
Gold Fools
Little Casino
The Moon in Its Flight

ESSAYS
Something Said

BIBLIOGRAPHY
Gilbert Sorrentino: A Descriptive Bibliography by William McPheron

FUNDER ACKNOWLEDGMENT

Coffee House Press is an independent nonprofit literary publisher. Our books are made possible through the generous support of grants and gifts from many foundations, corporate giving programs, individuals, and through state and federal support. Coffee House Press receives general operating support from the Minnesota State Arts Board, through an appropriation by the Minnesota State Legislature and from the National Endowment for the Arts, a federal agency. Coffee House receives major funding from the McKnight Foundation, and from Target. Coffee House also receives significant support from an anonymous donor; the Buuck Family Foundation; the Bush Foundation; the Patrick and Aimee Butler Family Foundation; Consortium Book Sales and Distribution; the Foundation for Contemporary Performance Art; Stephen and Isabel Keating; the Lerner Family Foundation; the Outagamie Foundation; the Pacific Foundation; the law firm of Schwegman, Lundberg, Woessner & Kluth, P.A.; Charles Steffey and Suzannah Martin; the James R. Thorpe Foundation; West Group; the Woessner Freeman Family Foundation; and many other generous individual donors.

This activity is made possible in part by a grant from the Minnesota State Arts Board, through an appropriation by the Minnesota State Legislature and a grant from the National Endowment for the Arts.

MINNESOTA
STATE ARTS BOARD

NATIONAL
ENDOWMENT
FOR THE ARTS

To you and our many readers across the country, we send our thanks for your continuing support.

Good books are brewing at coffeehousepress.org